The head coach blew his whistle for the next receiver to take off.

Billy waited, eyeing his target as the boy sprinted upfield. Then he reached back and cocked the ball by his ear in a sharp, compact motion. As the receiver cut, Billy stepped up and turned his body, bringing his arm forward. Like hammering a nail, Billy's wrist snapped automatically and the ball rocketed out of his grasp. The pass whistled across the field, spiraling beautifully, then bounced off the receiver's hands.

"Ow!" the back shouted. "I think you broke all my fingers!"

"It's only a ten-yard sideline pattern, Billy," Doc reminded him. "Take it easy on these guys."

"Right," Billy answered. But as he readied himself for the next throw, he saw Doc smiling.

ROOKIE QUARTERBACK

Paul Nichols

BALLANTINE BOOKS ● NEW YORK

To everybody.
We're all in this together.

Blitz

RLI: $\dfrac{\text{VL: 6 \& up}}{\text{IL: 6 \& up}}$

Copyright © 1988 by the Jeffrey Weiss Group, Inc.

Produced by the Jeffrey Weiss Group, Inc.
133 Fifth Avenue
New York, New York 10003

Library of Congress Catalog Card Number: 88-91547

ISBN 0-345-35108-8

Manufactured in the United States of America

First Edition: November 1988

ONE

Billy Tibbs walked out of the mid-August heat, and paused by the doorway to let his eyes adjust to the dimly lit locker room. Even though it had been empty all summer, it still smelled like dirty socks. A lot of guys were already changing for the first practice, and Marshall Danfield, Tucker High's punter and place-kicker, was telling one of his long, strange jokes.

"So the cow says, 'No way,' " Marshall said, looking around. " 'That's not a UFO, that's my mother.' "

Billy grinned. A couple of guys sitting near him burst out laughing, but everyone else just looked puzzled. Matt Kildare, the big senior wide receiver, took the opportunity to burp loudly. Just then, Assistant Coach Dunheim strode in the back door from the practice field. "Why is it," he asked, looking directly at Matt, "that it's always the ugliest guy on a football team who thinks burping is funny?"

"It wasn't me, Coach," Matt protested. "Anyway, I'm not ugly." He swept back a shock of black hair dramatically and posed for a moment. "I've got *character*. It must've been Danfield."

"No, it wasn't me," Marshall said. "But if we're talking ugly, I think Porter's our man."

Jeff Porter, the team captain, looked startled as he peered up from unlacing his shoes. He was quite handsome; Billy figured he could even be a model if he wanted to.

"Look at those ridiculously regular features," Marshall continued. "He could've been made in a test tube from a set of blueprints."

"You can't fit blueprints into a test tube," Jeff told him.

"Whatever. You get my point. I've found that girls prefer a true individual, someone with distinctive features—even a few so-called flaws."

"You've got plenty of those, all right," Matt agreed.

The whole team cracked up, and even Coach Dunheim chuckled. "There was a reason I came in here," he said loudly as the hubbub died down. "And it wasn't to enjoy your mature humor. Doc expects everyone out on the field in twenty minutes. No pads or helmets yet, but how about bringing your brains this year?" The coach pivoted and left.

Billy picked his way through the players toward his locker, and sat down on a bench next to Norm Jackson.

"If we had any brains, we wouldn't be here before school even starts," Norm said. The sophomore linebacker's locker was directly across from Billy's. Norm was dark and compact, sort of a three-quarter-scale model of a football player. He and Billy had been good friends since they'd played football together in junior high. "And I'll bet Dunheim spent the whole off-season thinking up that 'brains' comment," he added, sorting through a pile of clothes in front of him.

"I doubt it," Billy replied. "Give the guy some credit."

"I'm just not looking forward to this, you know? It's too hot for one of Doc's grueling workouts."

Billy nodded sympathetically. It wasn't going to be easy. Doc Samuels had been the head coach at the small school in northwestern Massachusetts for over twenty years. He was from the old school of coaching—hard work and hard knocks. If a player put out anything less than one hundred percent, he wasn't around too long.

"You know," Billy said as he began undressing, "Dunheim's right."

"Say what?"

"He's right. We do need to play smart this year. I mean, we're not going to blow away any teams with our size or experience, are we? What does that leave?"

"Speed?" Norm tried. He looked around the room. "Forget speed. How about cheating?"

"Brains."

"Luck?"

"We'll need that, too, I'll bet," Billy answered.

"Yeah, I guess you're right. Say, did you see

that interview of Doc in the *Herald* yesterday—
by that new guy?"

"Yeah." Billy grabbed his practice uniform
out of his locker. "I've never heard Doc sound
so negative about the team's chances. And we
haven't even started working out yet."

"Maybe it's reverse psychology or something," Norm reasoned.

"Are you kidding? Doc?"

"You're right. He doesn't even use regular
psychology." Norm pulled off his shirt and
kicked off his street shoes.

"You look like you gained some weight," Billy
said.

"I did. I've been lifting over at my cousin's."
Norm muscled up a bicep. "What do you think?"

A passing senior punched his arm. "Feels like
my little sister's," the older boy replied.

"Thanks. Appreciate your help," Norm called
over his shoulder. "Same old garbage," he muttered.

"Say, where's Tony?" Billy asked. Tony La-
Rico had played on the same junior high team as
Billy and Norm; the three had been close friends
for years.

"I don't know," replied Norm. "I talked to
him last night, and he said he'd be here."

The boys finished dressing in silence. Billy
wasn't looking forward to the practice any more
than Norm was. Doc's early workouts were brutal. And this year Billy had something to prove.
Carl Mulbrauer, a senior, had been the second-
string quarterback behind the record-setting Joe
King for the last three years. Now, with Joe
gone, Carl was expected to take charge of the

Tucker team. But Billy thought that he might
have a chance at the starting position himself,
and the best way to show Doc he had what it
takes was to excel in the first few practices and
workouts.

"We'd better get going," Norm finally said as
he finished tying his shoes. "Hey, look who's
here."

Tony had run in, already unbuttoning his shirt.
"Sorry I'm late, guys," he said. "You wouldn't
want to wait for me, would you?"

Norm and Billy laughed. "And risk Doc's
wrath? No thanks, we'll see you out on the
field," Norm said.

When Billy and Norm got up and headed for
the back door, most of the team began moving,
too. "Last one to the practice field is a rotten
egg," someone called, and a few foolish freshmen started running.

"Save your energy," Billy told a new kid near
him. "You'll need it."

A few minutes later, the team sat by the practice field at the far corner of campus and listened to Doc Samuels.

Doc was wearing his usual outfit: a white polo
shirt, gray shorts with a red stripe down the side,
black football shoes, and a Boston Red Sox base-
ball cap. "Welcome to Hell, boys," he began,
smiling briefly.

Some guys laughed nervously, and Billy heard
someone whisper, "There's his joke for the
year."

"Only thing is," Doc went on, "they don't
work as hard in Hell."

Everyone stopped laughing.

"So if you aren't ready to give me everything you've got, you might as well leave right now." Doc paused; no one left. "Some of you will quit later on, and that's okay. Not everyone's cut out for this."

Billy realized that he'd heard the same speech, almost word for word, the year before when he'd first gone out for football here at Tucker. He switched his attention from listening to looking.

Doc seemed older than last season. It wasn't that there were more wrinkles or lines on his face—there wasn't room for any more, anyway—but something about him was different. Billy studied the coach carefully. He was a well-worn, dark-haired man in his fifties, about medium size. His nose had been broken so many times that one of the team's traditions was to convince all the new players that Doc had played before face guards were invented. It might be the way Doc was standing that made him look older, Billy thought—kind of slumped a little more than usual. Or maybe there was just a little less life in his eyes, like he was tired before he even did anything.

Coach Dunheim stood behind Doc. He was a slender man with blond hair and a toothy smile—when he smiled. As head of the vocational ed program at Tucker, John Dunheim could be very tough in his own way. He wasn't like Doc; he didn't give orders in an old-fashioned style, but his message got through. Norm had told Billy about a disciplinary meeting with Dunheim once. It had been a megadose of reality. The coach had sat there smiling, telling him exactly what he knew about Norm's motives and fears—everything Norm was trying to hide.

"It was like he was a vicious shrink," Norm reported. "He never raised his voice, but, man, he blasted me."

On the other hand, if a guy was straight with him, Coach Dunheim would joke around, or cut a player some slack if he really needed it. A lot of guys on the team had problems with Doc, but very few disliked or disrespected Coach Dunheim.

A big man in his late twenties stepped up beside Doc as the head coach's speech ended.

"This is my son, Grant," Doc said, introducing him. "He'll be acting as an assistant coach this season, working mainly with the defense."

Grant Samuels raised a hand in acknowledgment. Billy knew that Doc's son had played a few years in the pros, and had recently moved back to town, but he'd never seen him before.

"I've talked enough," Doc said. "Get up and run the field perimeter twice, as fast as you can. It's a mile and a quarter. *Let's go!*"

Billy leapt to his feet and was among the leaders around the first corner. He wasn't big, but he was fast, and he would need his speed to even things up with Carl Mulbrauer. Carl was six feet three, two hundred ten pounds, and two years older. Billy glanced back and smiled as he rounded the second turn in third place. Carl was running near the back of the pack with the linemen. The senior had a decent arm, and a lot of poise for a guy that hadn't played much, but he sure was slow.

As the running began to hurt on the next

straightaway, Billy made a conscious effort to relax his upper body and establish a smooth rhythm. For a while, someone ran alongside him, trying to pass. Billy kept his head forward, concentrating on the ground in front of him, and eventually he heard the other guy's breathing grow raggedy. In another minute, the competition had dropped back.

It was hot; Billy was sweating freely at the halfway point, and the burning in his lungs grew worse, but he hung on to third place. He realized that he needed to catch his second wind—get beyond the pain—so he tried to concentrate on his chances of playing this year. He had an exceptional arm and was quick, but he knew his physical talents weren't his limitation. It was his lack of experience and leadership. Carl was a senior and this would be his fourth year on the team. Everyone respected his authority. Billy, on the other hand, was only a sophomore, and hadn't had that much playing time. He was quick and had a good arm, yeah, but nobody had confidence in his leadership—that's what it came down to.

As he entered the last turn Billy tried to focus on his performance again. His body screamed at him to slow down, but he knew he had to speed up to have a shot at winning the race. He was running second behind John Bucek, another starting wide receiver, with Matt Kildare in third place, talking a mile a minute about how much fun he was having. If it was a psych-out move, it was working on Billy. He couldn't have gasped a word if his life depended on it. And he knew that if he was close at the finish, Matt and John would both leave him in the dust. Matt was one of the fastest men in the Baldwin County conference, and John was a half-miler on the track team. So Billy gave it all he had and took the lead, trying to wear down the sprinters' legs behind him. He managed to stay in front until the final straightaway, but then Matt shot ahead of him easily, grinning, and John pulled up even. Billy fought him off for a few yards, but the older boy finally passed him. Then, just before the finish, one more runner got by.

Billy collapsed on the turf until Coach Dunheim made him walk. "Those legs are a blood pump, Tibbs. Your body's starving for oxygen and you need all the help you can get right now."

Billy nodded and staggered to the water cooler. He was satisfied with his showing in the run, he decided.

"Way to go," Norm told him, as he spilled a cup of water over his own head. "You beat all the running backs this year."

"Yeah," Billy wheezed. "A lot better than last year. How'd you do?"

"Above average, I guess. Not as fast as I need to be," Norm answered, dousing himself again.

"All right, Aquaman," Coach Dunheim said, clapping Norm on his back as he passed. "Let's get this show on the road."

The run was followed by stretching, then almost an hour of calisthenics. Some of the agility drills that were next would've been fun if everyone wasn't so tired. Finally, Doc ran the team again—wind sprints this time. That was the worst. The old coach stood on the sideline with a whistle. When he blew it once, everyone ran all out until they heard him blow it again. Then, after a very short rest, two whistle blows meant "get ready" and it was off again. Coach Dunheim yelled encouragement and moved around the field. Doc stood immobile the whole time, just blowing the whistle. It didn't even seem as though he was watching, although Billy figured he must've been. Doc made cuts after the first practice, and the sprints were where a guy's guts really showed. Billy was hard pressed to keep going all out, to get intense every time the whistle blew, but he knew that as a quarterback he needed to set an example.

Even armed with this point of view, Billy just barely managed to make it to the final whistle. His chest was on fire and his legs would hardly hold him up.

"Good-bye summer vacation," Norm groaned as the team trudged back to the locker room.

"Hello, Hell," Tony said.

John Bucek spoke next. "To paraphrase General Ulysses S. Grant: If I had my choice between here and the underworld, I'd live in Hell and rent out the damned practice field."

Ragged cheers greeted this pronouncement.

"I didn't know Grant played football," Billy heard one of the new kids say.

"Oh, sure," Marshall told him. "Doc was on the team with him—before face guards, you know."

The kid nodded, and Billy smiled. It was really football season again, all right.

TWO

The first week of conditioning seemed like a month, but finally Doc began the first skill-oriented practice on a gray, drizzly Monday. Billy noticed a small crowd on the sidelines as the team jogged out onto the practice field. He recognized most of the spectators as student scouts from the first few prep schools that the Tigers would play, but one of the guys looked older than the others and wore a white dress shirt and a red tie.

"Hey," Norm nudged Billy and gestured toward one of the bigger guys on the sideline. "Isn't that Kirk Tobin?"

"Sure is," Billy answered. Tobin was an awesome fullback for Dewey Prep. "I heard he started for Doc as a freshman—the only guy who ever did. But he got expelled, so his dad sent him to Dewey. He's trouble."

"The same Tobin as Tobin's Department Store?" Norm asked.

11

"Yeah. His little brother plays clarinet in the band."

"Sure. I know him. He's okay."

"Let's get moving," Doc brayed.

The team split up into three groups and Billy found himself with Coach Dunheim near the center of the practice field. His group was composed of offensive backs, receivers, and quarterbacks. Grant Samuels had the defensive backs at one end of the field, and Doc was working with all the linemen at the other.

"We're going to start by reviewing some basic techniques," Coach Dunheim told his group. "For example, all of you need to know how to block. It doesn't matter what your position is, or if you've been through this in previous years. So let's start with a shoulder block. Any volunteers?"

No one even twitched.

"Thanks, Chip," Coach Dunheim said. Chip Moorehead ambled forward sheepishly. He was the starting fullback, the biggest and strongest back on the team.

"I'll need one more victim," Coach Dunheim informed the group. This time, someone actually volunteered. Billy turned and saw it was Buck Young, a new guy who had recently transferred to Tucker as a junior.

"I'd rather hit someone than stand around," Buck muttered as he stepped forward.

"Great," the coach replied. "You be the blocker then, and Chip'll try and get through you. Then we'll talk about it." He lined the players up in front of each other. Chip and Buck both got down in a three-point stance. It was obvious to Billy that Buck didn't know what he was doing, but he definitely looked strong. Billy figured that chances were he wouldn't get hurt.

When the whistle blew, Chip came up hard out of his stance and Buck launched himself headfirst like a human projectile. They collided with a crash, then both players careened to the turf, Chip ending up on top of Buck.

"Get off me," Buck called, shoving his way free.

Chip staggered to his feet. "What hit me? Was that a train or what?"

Chip was swaying and stumbling, so Coach Dunheim sat him down on the wet turf while Buck swaggered back to the group of players and took off his helmet. His dark brown eyes issued a constant challenge, which the rest of him seemed eager to back up.

"Well . . ." Coach Dunheim began. "I've got no problem with the intensity level here, that's for sure. But let's look at the technique. Buck, why do you think they call it a shoulder block?"

"I guess you're supposed to use your shoulder."

"Right. Leading with your helmet is called 'spearing' and it's a penalty."

"It works pretty good, though, don't it?" Buck answered, grinning.

The coach nodded. "Right up until you break the vertebrae in your neck. Or paralyze the kid you're hitting. There are reasons behind the rules in this game. Now that you know, I'm sure that's the last time we'll see that." He paused and stared at Buck, who stared right back at him for a moment, and then nodded.

"There's a couple of things wrong with that block," the coach continued. "You didn't fire straight out—you were aimed downward. That's why you ended up on the ground with Chip on top of you. And you want to be able to sustain the block, keeping your footing, driving your man back. You want to stay in control the whole time, got it?''

Coach Dunheim looked around to see if anyone had any questions. "Okay," he continued, "let's try it. We can talk more about blocking after we do it awhile."

Billy was paired up with Chip, who was by now feeling okay after taking Buck's hit. They both already knew how to block, so they went about their business without much supervision. After a few minutes, Chip nudged Billy in the ribs.

"Hey, look." It was Buck jogging down to where the linemen were working with Doc. "I figured they'd put him in the line," Chip said. "We need a real aggressive tackle this year." He nailed Billy with a forearm that swept him off his feet. "Sorry about that."

It was rough, but Billy was enjoying the contact. Each collision was something real that penetrated his worries and thoughts to someplace more primal in him. It felt good to put aside all the normal niceties and just smash and be smashed. It was pure experience, too intense and basic to be anything else. Billy knew that some guys on the team didn't see it that way. Right near him, a couple of guys were drilling timidly, as though a real hit would be too impolite. He knew from experience that these guys were more likely to get hurt than he was. Doing things halfway made you vulnerable. Glancing around, Billy noticed that most of the other blocking pairs were going at each other enthusiastically. That was a good sign. You had to have football players that liked to hit—even more so on defense. At least this year's team looked good on that front.

After an hour and a half of blocking, ball-handling, and stance, Coach Dunheim and Doc switched groups.

"We're going to run pass patterns," Doc announced, squinting as though it were sunny instead of overcast. Billy, Carl, and a freshman named Dave "somebody" lined up to throw. They were starting with a ten-yard square-out, a pass pattern that had the receiver cut to the sideline about twelve yards downfield. Carl was up first. He seemed calm, not intimidated at all by the situation. His brown eyes scanned the field and he rubbed the football methodically. Even the way he stood impressed Billy. Carl held himself upright, but he was loose, too—on balance. Billy watched him carefully, trying to be objective in his evaluation of the older boy's performance.

Carl's first pass was on the money, and Matt Kildare hauled it in smoothly. His second throw wobbled and was slightly overthrown. Billy noticed that Carl used such a long windup that he had to begin his motion way before the receivers even cut. And on a drizzly day like this, with unsure footing, he was having to guess where they'd be. Sometimes it worked, sometimes it didn't. Billy also noticed that Carl didn't always hold the ball the same way. As Billy stepped up to pass, he heard Doc talking to Carl about his grip.

Then the head coach blew his whistle for the next receiver to take off. Billy waited, eyeing his target as the boy sprinted upfield. Then he reached

back and cocked the ball by his ear in a sharp,
compact motion. As the receiver cut he stepped
up and turned his body, bringing his arm forward.
Like hammering a nail, Billy's wrist automatically
snapped, and the ball rocketed out of his grasp.
The pass whistled across the field, spiraling beautifully, then bounced off the receiver's hands.

"Ow!" the back shouted. "I think you broke all
my fingers!"

"It's only a ten-yard sideline pattern, Billy,"
Doc reminded him. "Take it easy on these guys."

"Right," Billy answered. As he readied himself
for the next throw he saw Doc smiling. He had
really whipped that first one, and it felt great. The
next few passes were a little off as he adjusted to
throwing three-quarter speed. Then he found the
groove, firing the ball exactly where he wanted.
Much too quickly he had to give up his turn to the
freshman, whose footwork was so bad he actually
fell over several times. No threat there, Billy figured. He felt excited and pleased with himself as
he waited his turn. Not a bad start at all, he figured. He knew he was looking better than Carl
right then.

Perhaps Doc understood that a little fun was in
order, or maybe he just wanted to look over the
passing game carefully, but in any event, his group
spent the rest of the practice running patterns.
This suited Billy just fine, especially when he could
really unload on the deep patterns. At one point,
he dropped the wet ball, picked it up and hit his
man a good fifteen yards deeper than he'd planned
to. The ball must've traveled forty yards.

"Faster than a speeding bullet," Marshall Danfield crowed from his place on line. When he wasn't kicking, he was a backup wide receiver.

"More powerful than a locomotive," somebody else piped in.

"Knock it off," Doc warned, adding, "Nice throw, Billy."

But when the sophomore quarterback's turn was through, Doc still found things to correct. "Release the ball higher," he barked. "Loosen up on the follow-through." Sometimes Billy figured that if he ever did it exactly the way Doc wanted, the old man would tell him to tie his shoes some different way or blink more often. Doc Samuels was a hard man to please.

Back in the locker room, Billy was taking off his pads and talking to Norm when Doc came up to him with the young man with the red tie who had been watching the practice from the sidelines. The stranger was young, maybe college age, and short. He wore glasses, too, and his wide-eyed expression was exaggerated by the magnification of his lenses.

"Hi, guys," he said in an energetic, warm voice.

Billy, Norm, and a few other guys nearby nodded as Doc introduced the man.

"This is Stan Flender. He's the new sports reporter at the *Herald* and he'd like a few words with some of you media sensations."

For a moment everyone was quiet. By the end of last season, the old sports reporter at the *Herald* had labeled the Tigers "losers" in no uncertain terms. This had hurt; the whole team was relieved when the old-timer retired during the off-season.

"Specifically, he'd like to talk to you, Billy. Billy Tibbs, this is Stan Flender. I'll be in my office if you need me." Doc turned and strode off as the reporter called out, "Thanks, Coach."

By now, a large group of players were huddled around Billy's locker.

"Does an audience make you nervous?" the newspaperman asked.

"I guess so, but that's all right," Billy answered. "This is the first time I've ever been interviewed and I'd be nervous no matter what."

"With an arm like that, you'd better get used to attention."

"Did you watch practice?" Billy asked.

"I sure did." Stan Flender smiled. "You guys look like a pretty good team to me."

"Hey, this guy's all right," Norm exclaimed. "Are you going to put that in the paper?"

"Yup." Flender sat on the bench next to Norm, facing Billy, and pulled out a small spiral notebook. "Now I'd like to ask a couple of questions, Billy, and you just do your best to answer them honestly, okay?"

"Sure."

"What do you think the team's chances are this year?"

"I don't know exactly. We've got some real good players—like Matt Kildare, John Bucek, Chip Morehead, uh . . . Jeff Porter, and . . . Jim Grover, and lots of others. But I guess there's some spots where we don't have much experience."

"What do you see as the main problem, then? Experience?"

"Yeah—and size."

"Thanks, Billy."

"That's it?"

Flender laughed. "We'll do the two-hour interview after you win the state championship with one of those bombs.''

"He just might," Norm replied.

"We'll see," Flender answered as he rose. "Now can someone point me at Jeff Porter? I don't see why you guys don't wear numbers right on your skin. It would make life a lot easier for me.''

When the reporter had left, Norm slapped Billy on the back.

"You did great. You really must've impressed him out there.''

"It went pretty good, Norm. For the first day throwing, anyway.''

"All right! Keep it up. Only next time, I think you should mention my name. You know, like 'one of the real mooses on the squad is Norm Jackson. I sure feel good when he's in there.' ''

"I think it's meese," Tony LaRico chimed in.

"It's moose," Billy said.

"Sure it is," Norm replied. "When there's one. Then it's mooses for a whole flock of them.''

"Herd," Tony said. "A flock's a bunch of birds.''

"Whatever. This is a media sensation here, Tony. Let's not get off the topic. The point is, my man here is headed for big things.''

"Knock it off, Norm," Billy complained. "It doesn't matter what Flender thinks. It's Doc that matters.''

"Media pressure. Popular opinion. Do these words mean anything to you?''

Billy nodded wearily. The excitement was wearing off and he was too tired to argue.

THREE

After two weeks of practices, it was finally the morning of the first day of school. Billy hadn't exactly been looking forward to it, but now that September was here, it felt all right. He'd put in long hours on the practice field, handing off thousands of times, doing finger push-ups in full equipment—surviving all of Doc's torture tests. For that matter, he'd spent long hours off the field, too, studying his playbook. He was just as happy to switch over to regular studying and shorter practices. And Tucker High had something that the football team didn't. Girls.

It was a beautiful, sunny morning and the sidewalks around the school were crowded with students. Billy's eyes were drawn to the half of the population that didn't look like football players. They were his favorite thing about high school, although he got pretty tongue-tied around girls his age. If they were older or younger, he was okay. Billy figured that only potential dates made h'm really nervous, but at school this was nearly everyone female.

There was a tradition at Tucker that freshmen had to use the back door for the first week. A bunch of linemen from the team stood shoulder to shoulder in the school's front archway, moving aside if they knew someone or received proof of upperclassmanship. Not many kids had to show I.D.; it was a small school where almost everyone knew everyone else. And none of the freshmen were ever interested in tradition busting, anyway. Especially not when Brad Palmer, Elwyn Brooks, Jim Grover, and Ray Burroughs were the "bustees." Ray was the biggest guy on the team. He greeted Billy with creative swearing.

"What was that for?" Billy asked.

"General principle. We haven't had much chance to act ornery this year."

"It's just as well," Jim pointed out. He was the straightest guy on the team. With very short dark hair, and the wire-rim glasses he wore off the field, he didn't look like a football player at all. But he was pretty big by Tucker standards, and a good tackle that played both ways.

"You guys are lucky that Buck Young isn't a freshman," Billy pointed out.

"That's the truth," Elwyn agreed. He was Jim's buddy, a real naive, innocent sort of guy.

"We'd need a steel wall," Ray said. "That guy can go through concrete."

"I hear he's got your spot on the team, Brad," Billy told the senior guard.

"Like hell," Brad Palmer replied.

"He's just ribbing you," Jim told him.

Billy had picked Brad to spring his comment on, since his position as guard was completely secure. "Doc told me that he wants you to be the Tiger this year," Billy reported with a smile. "Said he wants someone who can really fill out that old costume for a change."

Brad grinned back at the sophomore. "So Doc's confiding in you now, huh?"

"Sure. You know what being a quarterback is like, right? It's an executive position. Carl and me consult with the coaches all the time."

The linemen grinned. Ray pushed Billy through the door. "Get in there and stay out of trouble, Tibbs."

"Sure thing. Take it easy, guys."

Billy moved into the busy school corridor, feeling on top of the world. That was the first time he'd ever successfully kidded around with older guys from the team. It looked like things would be different this year.

Tucker High School was composed of two main buildings, both two-story and brick. The "new" building was only twenty years old—the "old" one, seventy-five years old. It was bad luck to be assigned a locker in the old building, where nothing worked right. The lockers wouldn't open and the water fountains might refuse to flow at all or might shoot like geysers up your nose. There was no telling.

The crowded hallway in the old building was cinder block, painted that institutional green color that some prehistoric psychologist must've decided was soothing to students' brains or something. Billy had landed a locker in the new building this year, but his homeroom was near the girls' gym in the old one. That was typical school procedure, he thought as he headed toward his homeroom. They maximized the distance between two things you needed to do. Then, if you were late, no one could understand why. Typical.

Ms. Bertel's homeroom was also green cinder block, although she had put up a bunch of travel posters, which helped. She was a French teacher, though, so they were all photos of France. There were posters of French churches, French castles, French farms, and French beaches. It was ridiculous.

When Ms. Bertel handed out schedules, Billy wished he really was in France, or anywhere else besides Tucker High. He was taking algebra, English, American history, Spanish, biology, study hall, and gym classes, in that order, and he didn't like the looks of it at all. Algebra first thing in the morning. And lunch in between Spanish and biology. The gym period, which should've been like a vacation between the other classes, was wasted as seventh period. And the study hall was sixth; he couldn't use it to prepare for any of the day's classes. They couldn't have designed a worse schedule if they'd tried! Billy moaned and put his head down on his desk.

"Trouble?" a girl's voice asked. Looking up quickly, he saw it was Jennifer Saltz, a dark-haired girl who lived in his neighborhood.

"It's my schedule," Billy answered. "It's awful."

Jennifer leaned over from the adjoining desk to look at his card. Billy could smell her long, straight hair, and her shoulder touched his as she pointed at his schedule. He could scarcely get his breath.

"Look," she said, "we've got English and history together. I'm so bad in history, it's pathetic. I mean, what's the point, anyway?"

"I know what you mean," Billy stammered, very conscious of how close she was.

"It's all wars and politics. A bunch of grown-up boys acting out their hormones," Jennifer continued.

Billy grinned. "Well," he said, "it's better than English. That's my weakest subject."

"Don't you like to read?"

"Sure, but you don't read literature, you *study* it. You *talk* about it. You *write papers* about it. That ruins it completely."

Jennifer nodded sympathetically, but before she had a chance to speak, the announcements began over the intercom. Billy barely heard them. Jennifer seemed to like him; he wondered if he should ask her out.

When homeroom ended, though, she was out the door ahead of him, waving a good-bye and smiling a very pretty smile. Oh well, he knew he'd see her again soon.

On the way to his first class, Billy ran into Tony LaRico, who was heading to the same section of algebra. "Did you see the paper this morning?" Tony asked.

"No, why?"

"There's an article that really rips the team. Says we're still losers and always will be."

"You're kidding. Flender seemed like a really nice guy," Billy told his friend.

"Well, there's no name on it, but most guys I've talked to think it's gotta be him. I mean that other guy quit, right?"

"I sure hope it wasn't Flender," Billy mused aloud as he walked into class.

Tony nodded angrily. "We don't need another year of that crap."

The morning passed quickly. Billy's classes weren't as bad as he'd thought they'd be. Mr. Thomas, his history teacher, was a really funny guy, and Norm turned out to be in his Spanish class, and they both had lunch together right after that.

As usual, the cafeteria was jammed when Billy and Norm walked in. It was a long, high-ceilinged room that always smelled a little like garbage, no matter how clean it looked. Some kids said it was the food itself that smelled bad, but Billy didn't buy that. The food tasted all right to him. What bugged him about the odor was that he was getting conditioned to being hungry when he smelled it. He wondered if he would go through the rest of his life salivating when he walked by trash cans.

Billy and Norm had to wait forever on line to get their meals, and there were only a few seats left by the time they'd paid at the register. They were headed toward a table near the window when Carl Mulbrauer called them over to two long tables where a bunch of guys from the team were sitting.

"Shove over," Carl told the others. "Make some more room, would you?"

Billy and Norm tried to act cool about the invitation, but it was obvious that they were excited and pleased. The rest of the guys were angrily discussing the critical newspaper article.

"Just who does that punk Flender think he is?" Ray Burroughs demanded.

"Look on the bright side," Jim Grover answered. "It's another chance to be ornery."

"Who needs it?" Ray said, shoveling turkey pot pie into his mouth.

"Not me," Marshall Danfield replied. "School's got me ornery already after only four hours." The slim kicker shook his head sadly.

"Well, what can anyone expect from a permanent loser?" Matt Kildare pointed out.

"Who says I'm a loser?" Marshall asked, pretending to be angry.

"Flender does, you idiot," Matt replied.

"Oh, yeah. I'm so ornery, I forgot," Marshall told him.

"What I want to know is, what are we going to do about this?" Carl asked. His tone of voice was serious, and the mood at the long table changed.

"What can we do?" Chip Moorehead asked.

"We could refuse to talk to him anymore," Billy suggested.

"Or get up a petition to have him reassigned," Jim said.

"Or beat him up," Ray muttered.

"That's the one I like," Norm replied from his seat next to Billy.

"Maybe we should bring it up at practice," Carl suggested. "The whole team ought to be in on this."

"Yeah, that's true," Matt agreed. "The important thing is that we can't let that creep walk all over us.''

"Right," Carl replied.

"I'd hate to be in his shoes," Marshall remarked between mouthfuls of something yellow. "Hell hath no fury like a football player scorned."

"Amen," Norm agreed. "Let alone eighteen of them."

Later, during study hall, Billy sat by a window overlooking the parking lot. Although it was only the first day of school, someone was already making duck noises, and the teacher, who was clearly new, didn't know how to deal with the situation.

"Now, people," she called futilely. "Let's settle down."

Sometimes Billy wondered if they taught all new teachers the same dumb phrases. He'd been hearing about "settling down" for ten years now.

"All right!" the teacher shouted. "That's enough!"

Billy tried to tune out the chaos and concentrate on reading the poetry his English teacher had assigned, but it didn't work. He stared out the window and daydreamed instead. He was deep in his own territory, with two minutes to play, and the Superbowl on the line. Just as he dropped back to pass, an orange tiger ran by. An orange tiger? Billy focused on the scene in the school parking lot outside his window. The Tucker Tiger was loping across the asphalt. Whoever was in the moth-eaten suit wasn't much of a runner, though. It was probably some guy that hadn't made the band, Billy figured. He couldn't imagine why the mascot would be out in the parking lot during regular school hours, though. It was strange. As the figure ducked into a doorway, Billy thought he noticed something familiar about the way he moved, but just then the teacher yelled again. With a start, Billy's attention returned to the classroom. The teacher was telling the students that the next duck-noise person was heading to Mr. Muscatini's office.

"And, as I'm sure you all know, our principal is not one to skimp on discipline," she added.

"What *does* he skimp on?" someone yelled.

"Who said that?" the teacher shouted.

Eventually, the teacher stomped out of the room, presumably for reinforcements, but the bell rang before she got back.

After the last period, Billy decided to sit on the gym bleachers and try to read poetry during the activities hour. Most guys on the team left campus to grab a snack at one of the nearby hangouts. But Billy usually studied from three until the four o'clock practice, maybe munching on a piece of fruit he'd saved from lunch.

He hadn't been reading long when he was joined by John Bucek, the senior wide receiver and defensive back who would be going to Harvard next fall. He'd be the first Tucker graduate to enter the Ivy League in the last seven years. John was slim, but well-muscled, with black hair and blue eyes. This unusual color combination highlighted a handsome face, but Billy had noticed that Bucek didn't seem interested in parlaying his looks into a social life. He seemed more comfortable on the outside, making sarcastic remarks and showing everyone he was smarter than them.

"Hey, Tibbs," Bucek greeted. "You've found my private study hall, eh?"

"I guess so."

The senior sat near Billy, stacking a large pile of books in front of him. "Did you hear about Flender's car?" he asked. "Somebody Jackson Pollocked it."

"Huh?"

"Someone in the Tiger suit tried their hand at abstract art on the guy's wheels."

"You're kidding. I saw the Tiger in the parking lot during study hall," Billy told Bucek.

"Yeah?" Bucek asked. "Well, whoever was in that costume is gonna catch it at practice. You can count on that."

Later, when the team assembled on the field, the newspaper article and Flender's car were hot topics.

"It's a mess," Tony reported to Norm and Billy. The boys lay in the grass, waiting for the coaches. "It's a black Camaro, and there's yellow paint all over the grille and hood."

"He had it coming," Norm asserted.

"I don't know about that," Billy said. "There's freedom of speech, after all."

"This was freedom of paint," Norm said. "Same principle."

Suddenly, the players around them stopped talking, and Billy turned his head to see why. The three coaches were walking to the field, accompanied by Principal Muscatini, Stan Flender, and a black police officer.

"It's gonna hit the fan," Norm whispered as the men reached the team.

Doc spoke first. "We've got a situation on our hands. There's been an act of vandalism on school grounds and we have reason to believe that a team member may have been involved. Mr. Muscatini will elaborate."

The principal stepped up, a burly bear of a man with dark hair and even darker, bushy eyebrows. He was normally the team's biggest fan, but today his expression was fierce.

"First of all," he began, "let's get one thing straight. No criminal acts will go unpunished at Tucker High. None. The police are here and the vandal or vandals will be caught. I expect your cooperation. Any information about this crime can be dropped into the school suggestion box with complete confidentiality."

During all this, Stan Flender stood to the side with his arms crossed. He didn't appear to be sorry or mad or anything else.

The principal paused a moment, seeming to stare into each player's eyes. "The really stupid thing about this is that Mr. Flender didn't even write that article. I'll let him explain that part."

Flender spoke from where he was standing. "The *Herald* apologizes for the article, which was completely unfair. We're going to run a retraction tomorrow. We've got a new setup man and he mixed up the copy. What got in the paper was a letter to the editor. I've got to admit it looked more like an article than mine did—I don't type too neatly." Flender's expression tightened up and he looked down at the ground. He was even shorter and slighter looking with his head bent. Then he snapped his head up, his eyes blazing. "But I want you guys to know that I'm really angry about my car. If you've got a gripe with me, come deal with me. Don't take it out on innocent, inanimate objects. I'll probably write something you won't like sometime. You can talk to me about it and I'm willing to listen, but basically it's your problem. I'm not going to be intimidated out of writing what I see fit. Now I'm willing to put this incident aside and get on with my job. I'm not satisfied personally that it was any of you, and anyway, I don't live in the past. So let's say we start over."

"I have to say something, too," Doc broke in. "If I find out that anyone on the team knew something about the vandalism, and failed to speak up, he can forget about playing football."

Billy thought about who it might have been in the Tiger suit, but he had to admit he really didn't know. What bothered him was that it must have been someone from Tucker—probably someone on the football team who was angry over Flender's article. Billy didn't like the idea of possibly getting a teammate in trouble, but after wrestling with his conscience all through practice he finally approached Officer Neal on the sideline. He mentioned that the Tiger had looked familiar, but that he couldn't think why. "I know it looks like someone from the team did it," Billy told the policeman, "but it wasn't. I know how everyone runs. The strange thing is his stride *did* look familiar."

"We've got some evidence that points to a

team member," the policeman told him. "These sorts of things aren't always done by juvenile delinquents or troubled kids. It's an emotional reaction. Sometimes by someone like you."

"Me?" Billy gulped.

Officer Neal smiled. "Don't worry, Billy. You're not a suspect. Thanks for your help."

When he returned to practice, Billy put the incident behind him. He was sure the police would sort it all out, and with the first intra-squad scrimmage coming up, he had enough to worry about right on the field. He'd be guiding the second team against Carl and the starters. It wouldn't be easy.

FOUR

The day of the scrimmage was warm, but not nearly as humid as the early practices had been. As the team stretched, Billy scanned the field and noticed the principal and some cheerleaders among the several dozen figures seated in the aluminum bleachers. Flender was watching, too, seated at one end of the bench. They still hadn't caught whoever it was who had vandalized his car, but he was just as friendly as he was before it happened.

Although a lot of guys on the B team would have to play offense and defense, Billy had been told to just play quarterback. As his team prepared to kick off, he jogged over to Grant Samuels on the sideline. Grant would be the second team's coach during the game, while Doc and Coach Dunheim would direct the first team.

Grant was a tall, powerful man with broad shoulders and huge biceps. He'd played on the

special teams of several NFL teams before wash-
ing out of the league a few years earlier. As a
college player, he'd been a big-name linebacker,
but he hadn't had the speed to break into a
steady pro job. Billy knew that most of the team
really liked him. Grant was the only coach that
insisted you call him by his first name, and he
made an effort to put the players at ease. But
for some reason, Billy had never been really
comfortable around him. There was something a
little spooky about Grant's eyes, as if they con-
nected to someplace buried, maybe a weird part
of the brain or memories better off forgotten.

"Let's go!" Grant called to his team.

A freshman kicked off and Roger Critchfield
gathered in the ball on the fifteen-yard line. The
junior halfback sprinted toward the left sideline
as his blockers formed a wall in front of him.
Tony LaRico managed to break through the line
of blockers, but Roger sidestepped him and
turned upfield. He tightroped the sideline for ten
yards and then was forced out at the forty-one-
yard line. Carl would be starting from a great
field position.

"Watch these guys carefully," Grant told
Billy. "Think about what plays you would call
in their position." The A team snapped the ball
for their first play. Carl backpedaled, turned,
and handed off to Chip Moorehead, who slashed
through the line for a four-yard gain. It was a
good play—safe, but effective. The next play was
an end sweep, with Roger Critchfield carrying,
but the defense read it perfectly and met the
ball carrier at the line for no gain. That left it at
third and six—a passing down.

Billy thought about what he would do in this situation. He had a lot of confidence in the square-out pattern, where a receiver cut to the sideline about twelve yards downfield. He figured he'd call that, with a dump-off to Roger if no one was open.

Carl took the snap and dropped back to pass, but his line only held for a moment before the rushers were on top of him. Just as he was getting hit, Carl tossed a screen pass to Chip. The big fullback accelerated up the middle and found daylight, but as he shifted the ball, it slipped out of his grasp and took a crazy bounce. From behind, the defensive pursuit zeroed in on the fumble, and a sophomore dove on the ball for the B team. First and ten on their own thirty-five; it was a great break.

"Go get 'em, champ," Grant said, slapping Billy across his shoulders.

Billy trotted out to the huddle, his heart pounding. He called the same first play that Carl had. He crouched behind his center and barked a "hut!," received the ball squarely in both hands, pivoted smoothly, and moved off the line. As his fullback ran by, Billy carefully placed the ball into the boy's arms. He had barely done so when Buck Young smashed into the runner, shoving him right into Billy. Buck drove the two back several yards before smearing them onto the turf. Billy struggled to his feet, trying to plan the next plan, but he was still stunned by the three-yard loss.

"Looks like Buck means business," someone said in the huddle. "Let's trap the sucker."

"Sounds good," Billy replied. "Thirty-two red on three."

The trap was designed to let the defensive tackle charge, so the guard could pull out and hit him from his blind side. The lineman that let Buck by would lead the play into the hole, with the halfback following. When it worked, it defused the defense's aggressiveness and gained good yardage, too.

Billy did his job well, and it was a pleasure to see Buck get knocked on his can. Norm came up from his linebacker spot, though, and really crunched the runner, so it was only a three-yard gain which just got them back to the original line of scrimmage.

Billy called the square-out next, and hit his wide receiver for a first down on the forty-eight-yard line. It was a well-thrown ball, right on the numbers.

But as the team huddled up for the next play, Billy realized he had no idea what to call. Not wanting to get penalized for taking too much time, Billy just blurted out a passing play. As he trotted to his position behind the center, though, he realized that the play he'd called was just the type of risk that Doc hated to take early in a game. The head coach believed in establishing a strong ground game, mostly in the interior of the line. Then, to keep the defense honest, he believed in certain, safe pass patterns. If you could get good yardage without taking risks, then why chance it? The play Billy called was to be used when Tucker was down by a lot late in a game. Even then, there were other options that Doc preferred. But Billy couldn't call audibles at the line with a ragtag scrimmage team. He was stuck with his decision.

Billy took the snap, turned, and ran back into the pocket. His protection held up for just a moment—the defense hadn't expected a pass—and then Ray Burroughs was breathing down his neck. Billy rolled out to his right, only to find Buck Young waiting for him. Desperate, he cocked and threw the ball on the run to where the receiver was supposed to be deep downfield. Then he was buried. A cheer from the small crowd of spectators let him know that something had happened, but he couldn't untangle himself in time to see what.

"Touchdown!" a teammate called. "Great pass, Billy!"

The B team exchanged exuberant high-fives as they ran downfield to mob the freshman end who'd scored. He turned out to be a cocky little guy.

"No problem, Tibbs," he told Billy. "You throw it, I'll catch it." His buddies wrestled him to the ground and he struggled to maintain his dignity. For once, Billy felt much older than another player.

The backup kicker missed the extra point and Billy headed for the sideline again.

"Why in the world did you call that play?" Grant demanded as Billy approached. "That was just luck—you know that, don't you?"

"I agree," Carl said from behind Billy. "Dumb luck."

"I know. Sorry, Coach. I just lost it in the huddle and said the wrong play."

"Oh well," Grant responded in a sarcastic tone. "Then I guess it's not your fault, huh?"

Puzzled, Billy frowned. Grant glared back at him and changed tactics. "That sounded a lot like an excuse to me," he growled, stomping off. Billy stood a moment and then sat down on the bench by himself to calm down. If he was going to be effective when he got back in the game, he needed to shrug off Grant's behavior.

After the kickoff, Carl mounted a ground attack that gradually marched the A team down the field. He mixed running wide with hand-offs up the middle, even keeping the ball and lumbering off-tackle once himself. In bites of four and five yards, the yardage accumulated until the starters called a time-out on their opponent's nineteen-yard line. Players flopped down on the grass, their helmets beside them. The team's manager lugged water out to both groups as Carl consulted with Doc and Dunheim on the sideline.

Grant Samuels walked over and sat next to Billy. "What would you do here, Billy?" he asked. His tone was friendly; apparently he wasn't upset anymore.

"Play-action pass," Billy answered.

"Well," the coach responded, "it would probably be effective, but why change something that's working so well?"

"I think you've got to keep the defense guessing," Billy explained. "If you do the same thing over and over, sooner or later the other team's going to figure out how to stop it. If you keep them guessing, they might not. Then you can still use the run in the fourth quarter."

"Do you think our defense will figure out how to stop the A team's ground game?" Grant asked.

Billy had to grin. "You've got me there, Coach. I sure don't know how. They're just bigger and faster."

"So maybe you need to be suspicious of your motives," Grant told him. "Maybe the reason you want to pass is coming from inside, not from the situation."

"You mean maybe I just like to pass, so my decisions are biased?"

"Exactly. It's not the worst thing in the world, but you need to know about it to maximize your performance."

Billy nodded thoughtfully; Grant might just be right. And if Billy was aware of this tendency, he could compensate and be more objective. Yeah, he thought, it made sense.

Carl huddled up the offense and called his play. Billy knew that although the senior quarterback had consulted with the coaches, they wouldn't have told him what to call. The point of the scrimmage was to see what the players could do.

Carl received the snap and handed off to Chip, who blasted off-tackle for six yards. The next play, a pitchout to Roger, netted another first down on the eight-yard line. Then Carl decided to try a little deception. He faked hand-offs to Chip and Roger, and gave the ball on the reverse to Matt Kildare. The fleet wide receiver skirted the stacked defense and glided untouched into the end zone. After Marshall Danfield kicked the extra point, it was seven to six for the starters.

Billy went back out after the kickoff, but the

first three plays he called weren't even good for
a first down. As the second-string punter came
out to replace him, Billy jogged back to a seat on
the bench next to Grant Samuels.

"What's going on out there, Tibbs?" Grant
asked.

Billy looked down. "I don't know. I just get
real nervous sometimes. It seems like there's no
time at all between plays. Suddenly I'm in the
huddle and everyone's looking at me, and I don't
know what to do."

Grant slid closer to him on the bench. "Maybe
if you got a play sequence in your head before
you went out there, you'd feel more comfortable. It's something to fall back on, and your
plays wouldn't always have something to do
with what's happening on the field, so they'd be
less predictable. You see what I mean?"

"Yeah. I think so," Billy answered.

Grant paused. "If confidence is a problem for
you, Billy, let me tell you this. You've got talent."

Billy turned and looked at Grant, whose small
brown eyes were a little more "there" than
usual. The big man continued.

"I mean it, Billy. You've got a great arm, good
speed, and good balance. That's more than
enough to be successful in high school football.
Just be patient with the mental part. The more
experience you get, the easier it'll get."

"Boy, I sure hope so."

Grant moved down the bench and began yelling at a sophomore lineman.

Turning back to the game, Billy saw Carl toss
a long pass that fell far short of his target. A few

plays later, it was half time with the score still seven to six.

The two teams flopped down out of the sun under separate bleachers. It was cool and dark, and once he'd settled in on a patch of crabgrass, Billy felt far removed from the rest of the world. The glare of everything beyond the bleachers was too bright for his eyes to make sense out of. It was just light with no details—like overexposed film.

Grant got up and stressed that the team wasn't executing their blocks or tackles properly, but even so it was a close game. "You've got to get it into your heads that you can win," he said. "Unless you really believe that, it won't happen. And I really want it, boys," he added. "You're the first team I've ever coached, and I'm itching to beat Doc. Let's push these clowns around. Let's show them who's boss."

The coach took off to consult with Doc and Dunheim, and the team relaxed for another fifteen minutes. As it turned out, it wouldn't have mattered if they'd rested all day.

The first team began the second half by forcing a fumble on the kickoff, and scoring two plays later. When Billy finally got a chance to run his offense, his runners were hit in the backfield, his pass protection was brushed aside, and more often than not, the plays went for losses. Carl and the A team scored on every drive, once with a nice sideline pass that John Bucek turned into a touchdown after some flashy running. It was a lopsided mess. With four minutes to go in the game, the score was twenty-eight for the starters and six for Billy's squad.

At that point, Doc made some changes, including switching Billy to the A team.

"Call running plays only," Doc instructed Billy. "And go mostly to the right."

"Right, Coach," Billy answered, more nervous than he'd been all game long. He ran out to the huddle, where the atmosphere was completely different than it had been on the frustrated B team.

"Hey, they sent us a kid," Buck announced.

"It's Billy the Kid," Marshall added.

The starters were loose, having fun.

"I hope he's quick on the draw," Matt said. "He'll only have twenty or thirty seconds to get a pass off on this team."

"Come on, guys," Billy pleaded. "Let me run things like I'm supposed to."

"Sure thing, kid," Buck answered. "Why don't you throw it to me one time."

"You're ineligible."

"So?"

"Look, here's the play," Billy replied, trying to take charge. "Fourteen green on two. Let's see some hitting."

"Yes, Coach," Matt quipped as the huddle broke up.

Billy took the snap, pivoted, and handed the ball to Chip, who went through the line for eight yards. What a difference, Billy thought. He called for a pitchout next to Steve Wainwright, who was in at halfback. The senior ran for four yards and a first down. For the rest of the game, Billy called running plays, and the A team marched down the field. A few guys kept calling him Billy the Kid, and some of the older players never let him feel like he really belonged with them, but all in all it was fun. When the final whistle blew, the starters were on the six-yard line and would've scored if there had been time.

"You blew that, kid," Buck muttered as they walked off the field.

Billy realized that the team didn't know he'd been told not to pass. They figured he'd just lost track of time or was too scared or something. The crowd gave one last cheer, and the Tigers headed for the showers.

Jeff Porter walked with Billy as they headed to the locker room. "You did fine, Billy," the team captain told him. "It's tough playing with the subs. They're just too inexperienced to get much done."

"Thanks, Jeff. It sure felt different playing with you guys."

"I hope so," Jeff replied. "Otherwise we're in even more trouble than everybody thinks."

Norm Jackson joined them as they neared the school building. "I was worried at half time," the sophomore linebacker reported. "Seven to six against the subs. You had us going, Billy."

"A fumble and a lucky pass—that's all it was," Billy replied.

"I know that," Norm said. "But they use numbers to keep score, y'know, and it seems to me we only had one more than you."

Billy frowned.

"You're not much at taking a compliment, are you?" Norm asked.

"Twenty-eight to six. Those are the numbers, Norm."

"Don't come down on yourself too hard," Jeff

interjected. "Joe Namath couldn't have won with that team."

"He's right, Billy," Norm agreed. "That's just the kind of negative attitude your dad's always talking about."

Billy jumped up and down in mock joy. "Yay!" he shouted. "Yip, yip, yip, yippee!"

From a vantage point several yards behind the boys, Coach Dunheim turned to Doc. "Football players get stranger every year," he commented.

"Everyone does," Doc replied.

FIVE

That night at dinner, Billy's family wanted to hear all the details of the scrimmage. Billy felt lucky that his parents were interested in and approved of his playing football. He knew that other guys' families weren't so supportive. Whenever Norm tried to talk to his mom about football, she clamped her hands over her ears and chanted, "violence, violence, violence" until he'd finished. Real helpful.

"So how did Norm and Tony do?" Billy's dad asked as he helped himself to the lasagne.

"Okay." Billy answered. "Norm's got himself a spot as linebacker on the first team, but it looks like Tony's going to spend a lot of time on the bench as a sub."

"That's not bad for a sophomore, though, is it?" Mrs. Tibbs pointed out.

Billy shrugged. "Maybe it's so tough because it's Norm that beat him out. He's just a sopho-

45

more, too, you know. Tony's pretty discouraged."

"Will you be playing a lot this year?" Billy's little sister, Alice, asked.

Billy laughed and mussed her red hair affectionately as he got up from the table. "I hope so, Alice. I hope so."

Later that evening, the phone rang while Billy was sprawled on his bed studying history. A minute later Alice ran into his room to tell him that it was Tony on the phone.

"What's up?" Billy asked.

"I forgot to ask you if you were going to the talk tonight," Tony said.

"What talk?"

"Didn't you hear about it? Some pro guy that Grant played with is a sports psychologist now. He's in town giving a lecture at the Vet's Hall. They announced it at practice."

"I don't remember that."

"The guy's name is Robert House and he was a tight end with the Giants," Tony explained. "He's supposed to be a real good speaker, though. He talks about the philosophy behind sports and all that sort of stuff. It's at eight o'clock and it's only two bucks."

"Hold on," Billy said. "Let me go check with my dad."

Mr. Tibbs was reading the newspaper in the living room. At first, he was reluctant to let Billy out on a school night, but when he heard Robert House's name, Mr. Tibbs's eyes lit up and his mood changed. "I've read about him," he told Billy. "He's supposed to be something really special. How about I go, too? I can drive you boys, and I'll even pay."

"It's a deal," Billy answered, surprised at his dad's reaction. He ran back to the phone and told Tony the good news.

The time passed slowly while Billy finished his homework. Finally, at twenty till, Mr. Tibbs called up to Billy that he was ready to leave.

The Tucker Veterans' Hall was an old brick building just off Main Street near Tobin's Department Store. It looked like a bricked-over Quonset hut, with a curved roof line and sets of double doors at either end. The flagpole in front, next to an old howitzer, was one of the tallest things in town. There was already a pretty good crowd inside when Billy, Tony, and Mr. Tibbs arrived. It looked like a lot of the team was there, and maybe forty or fifty others. Grant Samuels was sitting in the front row next to his dad, who introduced the speaker a few minutes later.

Robert House turned out to be an odd-looking character. He must've been six feet five at least, and every bit as muscular as Grant Samuels. But he had a huge, bushy beard that covered the bottom half of his face and the top half of his chest. It was like he was a football player up to a certain altitude, and then he turned into a mountain man. His brown hair was a little long, too, although Billy could look around the hall and see kids with longer hair. The other thing about him was that he gave an impression of being very calm. He may have been standing in front of a crowd, waiting to speak, but he seemed totally comfortable with the situation.

There just wasn't any tension or anxiety visible in his features. *I wish I could be that cool during games,* Billy thought.

"Thanks for coming," House began. He had a low, smooth voice. "I'd like to talk about time first. It's got a lot to do with sports, but not many people seem to understand it. We live in the present tense. Tomorrow doesn't exist—it's a concept. When we get to tomorrow, it's today. And yesterday is only in our heads, too."

For a moment Billy wondered if they'd come to the right lecture. This didn't sound like any sports talk he'd ever heard.

"Have you ever lost track of the time because you became deeply involved in doing something?" House went on. "When I used to run pass patterns for the Giants, if I thought about what had happened last play, or what might happen to me after I caught the ball, I didn't make the play. I wasn't the fastest tight end around, and I wasn't the biggest or most coordinated. My advantage was that when I ran a pattern, I ran a pattern. That was *all* I did. I tried to be one hundred percent focused on what was going on."

Tony nudged Billy and rolled his eyes, but Billy quickly turned back to the speaker.

"What I'm saying really isn't as weird as it sounds," House continued. "You all know concentration is important in sports performance. If you try to return a kickoff by keeping one eye on your blockers and the other on the cheerleaders, you don't score too many points."

The crowd laughed.

"So what I'm saying is, take that principle a

step further. It won't hurt to experiment; I'll even give you a tip on how to do it. You always do something in the present tense already, whether you realize it or not. Does anybody know what I mean?"

"Looking at cheerleaders!" someone shouted, and the crowd roared again. Robert House laughed the loudest and longest.

"That may be true," he finally conceded. "But I mean breathing; we're always breathing. If you pay attention to your breath, you're there with your breath, not off thinking about school or work. I used to do breathing exercises before every game so I could empty my mind of everything I didn't need." House paused and drank from a glass of water on the table next to him. "The thing is, our bodies know how to do things—especially after we've trained them. We need to learn how to get out of our own way. That's what it amounts to."

Billy liked that phrase—get out of your own way. He knew he was his own worst enemy on the field. As House continued to talk Billy began to feel better about solving his football problems. Maybe he could learn to live more in the moment and banish his nervousness.

The trouble began when the talk was over. Grant Samuels got up to shake his friend's hand, but was so drunk he could hardly walk. He fell over a chair and hit the floor hard, and didn't get up. It took three men to help him out of the auditorium.

"That's a man with a problem," Mr. Tibbs told his son.

Suddenly it struck Billy that Grant's "problem'' might account for his sudden mood changes, and the way his eyes looked funny sometimes. It all made sense. "That's Grant Samuels, Dad. The assistant coach."

"For now he's a coach," Mr. Tibbs finally remarked.

On the drive back, Tony began complaining about Robert House's lecture.

"What a crock," he pronounced. "That guy doesn't know anything. When he runs a pattern he runs a pattern. So what? Everybody's always wherever they are. And there's a yesterday and a tomorrow. That's not something to wonder about."

"I don't know," Billy protested. "I think he may be right about being in the present. I just don't know how to do it."

They pulled up to Tony's house, and the blond-headed boy spoke as he got out of the car. "Let that House guy try being 'fully present' on the bench. I'll bet he wouldn't think so much of reality from there."

"You might be right," Mr. Tibbs replied with a smile.

"Well, thanks for the ride and all. Good night, Mr. Tibbs. See ya tomorrow, Billy."

After Billy and his dad had begun to drive again, Mr. Tibbs spoke. "Tony sure is upset. I've never seen him like that. Is he having any problems?"

"I don't know. I think it's just football," Billy answered. "We work really hard at practice, and I guess Tony just isn't getting enough back."

"It must be rough for you, too, huh?"

"Yeah. But I'm all right." Billy thought about

it for a moment, then added, "I guess the difference between us is that I've got a real chance to play."

It was hard to concentrate at practice the next day. The weather was unusually hot, for one thing. And between the lecture, Grant's drunkenness, and the Tiger-suit crime, rumors were flying all over the field. During warm up, Billy heard that the whole team was going to be tested to see which eleven guys were most in the present. Then Norm told him that he'd heard that Grant, who was absent, was serving a two-year sentence for disturbing the peace.

"That's silly. He was drunk just last night and all he did was fall down."

"I'm just telling you what I heard, Billy."

"Hey, guys," John Bucek called. "I heard a good one. Someone told me that it was Grant in the Tiger suit and the Tiger was wearing a Grant suit last night."

"He's probably the guy making up all the rumors," Billy told Norm. "What a strange mind he's got."

The incident that really disrupted practice and shook up everyone occurred near the end of the passing drills. The receivers and running backs were working against the linebackers and defensive backs. Billy and Carl were passing. There wasn't a single cloud in the sky, and everyone was really sweating and gasping in the hot sun. In the middle of a play, Doc and Officer Neal strode onto the field, the coach blowing his whistle over and over. All across the practice

field, players stopped and watched. Doc was
wearing his usual Red Sox cap, polo shirt, and
shorts; his face reflected the rough night he
must've had dealing with his son. Now, as he
stopped by the linebackers, there was something
more on his face, too. He was angry. Billy had
never seen him so angry.

"LaRico!" Doc bellowed.

"Yes, sir?"

"This officer has something to say to you."

Tony ran up and pulled off his helmet. "Sir?"

"Tony LaRico?" the policeman asked in a for-
mal voice.

"Yes?"

"You're under arrest. The charge is second-
degree malicious mischief."

Billy listened unbelievingly as the policeman
began to read Tony his rights.

By now, Coach Dunheim had arrived on the
scene from the other end zone. "You're telling
me that Tony is your criminal?" he asked. Dunheim put his arm across Tony's shoulders. Tony
just stood there, too stunned to react.

"I'm satisfied with the evidence, John," Doc
replied.

"You don't really know this boy, do you,
Doc?"

"I know all I need to know," the older coach
answered. "When Officer Neal fills you in, you'll
see that we have no choice."

"Doc, I don't think that this is the time or the
place to discuss it," Coach Dunheim said. "Let's
get off the field and talk about this in private."

The two coaches stared at each other for an
uncomfortable length of time. Then John Dun-

heim turned and looked questioningly at the policeman.

"It's okay with me," Neal said. "Come on, son." He started to pull on Tony's arm, but Coach Dunheim pushed his hand away.

"That won't be necessary," the coach told him.

Tony turned to go and Billy caught a glimpse of his face. His eyes were filled with tears and his features were frozen in place. He stumbled off the field, moving like a zombie.

"Take a break," Coach Dunheim called to the other players as he departed. "We'll start up again in a few minutes."

The team was in a state of shock, with everyone milling around angrily. Jeff Porter yelled for everyone to gather up, and they did.

"The important thing is that we don't tear up the team taking sides or anything," Jeff began. "I don't know what's going on. I mean, maybe it's all a mistake or maybe Tony lost control and did it. I don't know."

"Well, I know," Norm asserted. "There's no way Tony did it, no matter what evidence they have."

"That's not the point he's making," Matt responded. "The point is that no matter what the truth is, we need to stick together."

"Exactly," Jeff agreed. "Let's just not argue about it. And by that I don't mean that I think Doc did right, or Tony's guilty or innocent."

"That's easy for you to say," Norm told the older player. "You're not his friend. There's no way I'm going to turn my back on Tony."

"Calm down, Norm," Jim Graves said. "We're all friends here."

"Well, I don't care," Norm continued. "I say Doc screwed up coming on the field with a cop. How'd you like to go through that?"

"Aw, he was just upset 'cause of Grant," Roger said.

"Shut up, Critchfield."

"Norm?" Billy said.

"Yeah?"

"Cool it. This isn't helping Tony or anybody else."

There was a pause and the tension subsided somewhat. Then Coach Dunheim returned alone and stood in front of the team.

"Men, I apologize. It didn't have to be like this. It's been a series of unfortunate circumstances from start to finish. Doc has gone with Tony down to the police station until his folks get there. Apparently, they've got a case against Tony and we'll just have to wait and see how strong a case it is."

"Is he still on the team?" Norm asked.

"That's Doc's decision, and I'm not going to get into that. What I will get into is the rest of practice. We've got a lot of work to do if we're going to succeed against Cranbrook."

The last half hour of practice was a complete waste of time. Guys were dropping passes, running the wrong plays, and tripping over their own feet. The final whistle was merciful.

What a way to go into the preseason, Billy thought. *It couldn't be much worse.*

SIX

It turned out that the police let Tony go right away, but he had to promise to return for a hearing. He'd been on his lunch period during the crime and because he'd been studying under a tree by himself, he didn't have much of an alibi. Also, someone saw Tony walk by the storage locker where the Tiger suit was kept, which Tony didn't deny—it was on the way from the cafeteria to the back door of the school. But the worst thing was that the police found flecks of yellow paint—the same kind as on Flender's car—on Tony's bicycle. It had been chained to the bike rack near the parking lot, and Tony told the police that whoever the vandal was must've splashed paint on it by accident, but they didn't believe him. Flender himself believed that Tony was innocent, but the police didn't seem to care about that, either.

Doc suspended Tony from the team until the

matter was settled. Tony turned around and quit, throwing his helmet onto Doc's desk, which made the coach furious again. Tony and Doc ended up shouting at each other like two kids, as the whole team listened from their lockers. Tony quit, then Doc cut him, then Tony said he couldn't get cut because he'd already quit, then Doc shouted that he was cut anyway. It was a mess.

Grant showed up at practices again, acting like nothing had happened, and nobody said anything to him about the night of the lecture. The defensive coach did his job the same as ever. He even spared some time for Stan Flender, who, as usual, was hanging around looking for a new angle on the team.

So the team tried to focus on the upcoming home scrimmage against Cranbrook. It would be an informal game, where coaches from either team could stop the action whenever they wanted. Supposedly, no one would keep score, although it was hard not to keep track in your head anyway. Especially when Cranbrook and Tucker would play for real, later in the season.

Coach Dunheim tried to put the game in perspective for the team, speaking in the locker room before Tucker took the field. "We're not ready to play a team like the Bulldogs, but they're here and we're sure going to try it anyway," he began. "I don't care if we score a lot of touchdowns and I don't care if they do. But I do care about executing the way we know we can—playing the best possible scrimmage at this point in the season. Okay?"

The team nodded, almost in unison, and for a

second Billy felt fine. Then, as the coach left, someone burped, and Matt told him to shut up. Ray spoke up then, telling Matt to stop being so negative. John Bucek pointed out that Ray was being negative, too, and they started to argue until Buck told them both to shut up.

"Wait a minute," Jeff interrupted. "Let's take it out on Cranbrook, not on ourselves."

"Yeah," Billy added, realizing that he needed to get involved if he wanted to be a team leader. "Let's kick around those Bulldogs."

"Let's leash them," Norm suggested.

"Let's curb those dogs," Marshall added.

"Let's pick them up by their ears," John said.

"Let's slap their little snouts," Matt tried.

As the team finished dressing, Matt, John, and Marshall kept listing increasingly ridiculous things to do to bulldogs. Billy figured that if the team couldn't unite for more than two seconds, then dumb jokes were a better way to pass the time than arguing. But when Marshall and some others carried rolled-up newspapers down to the field, Billy didn't think it was that funny. He had a game to play—one of only a few good opportunities to prove himself to the coaches—and he needed to make the most of it. Even though the plan was for Billy to play just the latter part of the first half, he wanted to get serious right at the start.

There were quite a few spectators in the new bleachers, and they cheered as the Tucker team arrived on the sideline. The team gathered around Doc in front of the middle bench, and Billy began breathing deeply, trying to pay attention to the way it felt. Doc gave virtually the same speech Dunheim had, with a few Doc-type phrases thrown in. Hardly anybody seemed to listen. And then the kickoff team ran onto the field, Tucker kicked off, and the scrimmage began.

Cranbrook wore navy blue jerseys with white trim. They looked awfully big as they formed a wall of blockers in front of their kick receiver. For their opening play, their ball carrier tore upfield behind his interference, busting loose at his forty-yard line, and getting to Tucker's forty-five before Marshall brought him down. When the kicker had to make the tackle, you knew you were in trouble.

Then Cranbrook's quarterback gave the ball to the same guy, who was in at halfback, and he sprinted around the right end for eight yards.

"Who is that guy?" Billy asked Chip Moorehead, who was sitting near him.

"R. C. Truman's little brother. He can scoot, can't he?"

"I'll say." R. C. had played several years ago and was still the conference's all-time leading receiver.

Next, Cranbrook's signal caller ran a quarterback sneak for three yards and a first down.

"You're not supposed to get three yards on a sneak," Billy complained.

"You are if your center's eight feet tall," Marshall answered. "Look at that monster."

"Whoa!" The Cranbrook player was the biggest high school kid Billy had ever seen.

On the next play, the fullback came up the middle. Jeff Porter managed to sidestep the giant center and meet the ball carrier head-on for only a one-yard gain. The Tucker bench erupted in cheers.

"All right!" Billy called.

"Kill their heads off!" Marshall shouted.

But that one play was the only highlight for the Tucker defense in the first quarter. Cranbrook marched down the field, never throwing the ball, and scored easily on an off-tackle plunge. After a successful extra point, a strong kick to Roger Critchfield gave Tucker its chance on offense.

Although Roger was smothered at the twenty-two-yard line, Carl gave him the ball on the first play, just as Cranbrook had with their halfback. The sweep went for four yards, which was a good start. Then Chip barreled up the middle on a trap play, which worked perfectly, except the safety came up fast and nailed him after four more yards. So it was third and two on the thirty-yard line.

From the sideline, Billy considered what he would do here. Maybe another hand-off to Chip up the middle. Even with Cranbrook looking for it, a well-executed fullback smash ought to get the yardage.

Carl called something better. He took the snap and moved to his right, with Roger moving behind him. But the big quarterback was too slow to make it work. As he hit the line, the middle linebacker adjusted his pursuit and met him with a bone-crunching tackle. Tucker was a half yard short of a first down and would have to kick.

The rest of the first quarter was more of the same, although both coaching staffs began interrupting the game between plays. When Cran-

brook had the ball, they ran for five or six yards
at a crack, eventually scoring each time. Tucker,
on the other hand, couldn't get a first down, although they came close a few more times. Between quarters, Doc took Billy aside to advise
him on his play-calling.

"You'll be coming in as soon as we get the ball
back, Billy, and here's what I want you to do.
Try a thirty-three pass pattern on the first play.
That should take them by surprise. Then send
Roger around the weak side on the halfback
counter. Now assuming this brings you to a third-
down situation, I want a quarterback draw. Let's
see that speed of yours. After that, you're on
your own."

"I'll do my best," Billy promised.

Billy entered the game a minute later, after
Cranbrook scored a touchdown and kicked off
again. First and ten on the eighteen. All the
starters were in except for Billy, and they stared
expectantly at him as he stood in the huddle.

"Thirty-three on two," Billy barked.

"Doc won't like that," Ray warned.

"He told me to call it," Billy answered. "Now
let's go."

On the line, poised behind Ray, Billy's heart
pounded, and his hands shook a little. The Cranbrook players looked much bigger from close up,
and it was hard to believe that he could do anything against them. Probably they'd sack him
right off, and he'd fumble or something. Great.
Just the thing to think about as he called for the
ball.

On two, he took the snap and dropped back
into the pocket. Before he knew what he was

doing, he'd fired the ball to Matt. The wide receiver gathered in the pass and was nailed immediately. Second and four. Billy called a weakside sweep for Roger and there was no discussion this time. The play was good for two yards before the halfback was forced out of bounds.

"We're rolling now," Jeff Porter declared in the huddle, but before Billy could call the next play, Doc and Dunheim came out on the field to talk about the blocking on the last one. When they'd gone, Billy spoke to the older guys surrounding him. "Seventeen red on three," he announced.

"Good call," Chip said.

"This'll get 'em," somebody else agreed.

And it did. The play worked beautifully. As the Cranbrook pass rush stormed the quarterback, Billy pump-faked deep and charged up the middle. He was past the line before they knew what hit them, and he managed to fake out one linebacker before another one took him down. It was an eight-yard gain—the most successful play of the scrimmage so far. Billy felt great as he huddled up the team again on the thirty-four-yard line. Cranbrook wasn't so tough he decided; he was sure he could score on them.

Billy called for Chip to carry the ball through the tight end's position. But Cranbrook blitzed and someone caught Chip on the ankle right after he took the hand-off. He shook free but had no momentum as he hit the line a little later than he should've. No gain; second and ten. Billy decided to go with a passing play next instead of waiting for third down. The other players nodded at the call, and Matt said, "Let's make it work" as the huddle broke.

Billy took the ball from Ray and backpedaled just a step. Matt wasn't open, but John was for a second, so Billy rifled the ball to him before the safety could get over on the double coverage. The ball hit Bucek in the numbers and bounced up. It was up for grabs, but no one could get to it before it hit the turf. Third and ten.

"Hey," John said to Billy as the next huddle formed. "Throw it harder next time, huh? I've still got a lung that isn't collapsed yet."

"I had to do that," Billy explained. "The safety was closing in on you."

"Don't justify yourself," Matt told him. "You're the quarterback."

"He's right, Billy," Jim Grover added. "You don't need to discuss things—you're in charge."

"So why are all you guys talking in the huddle if he's in charge?" Chip pointed out.

"That's right," Billy responded. "I'll do the talking. And we're going to have to hurry to get this play off, too. Uh . . . forty-two blue. No, make that forty-four blue. On two. No. Hold it a minute." It was happening again. Billy looked up at the faces around him. They were all staring at him, some with concern, some with disgust. "Ref!" the sophomore quarterback called. "Time out!"

The official blew his whistle, and Billy trotted to the sideline where Doc was standing.

"What the heck was going on in that huddle?" the coach asked.

"Aw, we were just talking about the last

play," Billy answered, turning red inside his helmet.

"You need to lay down the law, Billy. Nobody talks in the huddle but you."

Billy looked down. "Maybe you should tell them that," he said.

"They need to learn to listen to you," Doc replied. "It's not going to count for anything if someone else makes them pretend they respect you."

Billy nodded. "I understand. The thing is, I didn't get a chance to think of a good play while all that was going on. What should I do?" he asked Doc.

"Think about it now," Doc said slowly. "What's the situation?"

"Well, it's third and ten, so they'll be looking for a pass. But we're not going to get ten yards without passing, so I guess we ought to try one."

"Which pattern?" Doc asked.

"I don't know. Do you think it would be okay to go deep here? We're way behind and we've been setting it up with those shorter passes."

"It's up to you. Just be careful."

"Right." As Billy turned back to the field he saw Carl staring at him from the bench.

"Play forty-two on first sound," he told the offense back in the huddle. "And nobody else talks in the huddle anymore."

The team paused a moment, glancing around at one another, but no one said anything. Billy breathed a sigh of relief, the huddle broke up, and the play unfolded.

The pass rush was fierce, and Billy had to scramble out of the pocket almost immediately.

As he rolled to his right, ducking under a lineman's grasp, he spied Matt a step ahead of a Cranbrook cornerback. But right then another rusher forced him to dodge a tackle. When he'd wriggled free from someone else who'd grabbed his foot, Billy threw and gave it all he had. Unfortunately, while he'd been scrambling, the Cranbrook safety had cut over and put the clamps on Matt. Billy watched his pass head into the double coverage; the cornerback was just behind the receiver and the safety was just in front. Worse yet, the pass was too short. Although Matt leapt high to try and bat it away, the Cranbrook cornerback intercepted the ball and began sprinting upfield. Chip Moorehead tripped him up at midfield, but the damage was done.

Billy trudged to the bench and sat by himself. He had messed up badly and he felt like a fool. Jeff and Brad walked by to say "nice try" and "tough luck," but it didn't help. It turned out that that was all the action he saw, too. Cranbrook continued to stay on the ground, using up several minutes in a successful scoring drive. Then, on the kickoff, Roger coughed up the ball after a great runback, and Cranbrook cranked up its power offense again. Their quarterback timed the drive perfectly, going into the end zone on a sneak right as the first half ended. The score was probably twenty-eight to nothing or something. Billy didn't even want to know.

The three coaches talked a lot under the bleachers during the extended half-time break. Tucker still wasn't executing properly, John Dunheim stressed. Doing things right would counteract the size differential, he told the team. They needed to be where they were supposed to be, doing what they were supposed to be doing. Too many guys were getting lost, or reverting to bad habits in their tackling and blocking.

Doc scolded the defensive backs for their unaggressive play. "Are you guys waiting for invitations from the line?" he asked. "Or are you just enjoying covering receivers when there aren't any passes? It's easier than usual, isn't it? You've completely shut down their passing game. Great. Now, let's see some hitting up at the line."

Doc had some words for the offense, too. He wasn't pleased at all by the intensity level. "Cranbrook's just playing harder," he said. "That's all there is to it. And all things being equal, that's all it takes. The problem is, all things aren't equal. Cranbrook is bigger and more experienced, so if we aren't more intense than they are, the second half is going to be a waste of time. I'd rather have you guys running laps than going through the motions on the field. If I don't see more effort, I'll just stop this so-called game and we'll have a little track meet. Understand?"

Grant mostly yelled at the defense for not hitting harder. He picked on a few players, too, including Norm. And then he said that Billy had no excuse for throwing that interception.

"I didn't say I did," Billy answered. He was the first player to speak during half time, and he could see that he surprised a few people by responding. "It was a bad pass—a bad idea. I'll accept responsibility for that."

"You'll have to," Grant answered. "There's nobody else to blame."

"And I'm not blaming anyone else," Billy persisted.

"Look," Coach Dunheim interrupted. "One play doesn't account for all our problems, and we're better off resting than talking, so take ten minutes, and then let's see something different."

It was different. Worse. Tucker played harder, but Cranbrook opened up their offense and unleashed a potent passing game. On defense, they began stunting and blitzing, and Carl was too slow to stay out of the grasp of the Cranbrook rushers. Chip broke free for one great run, nearly scoring, and Matt and John managed to get open quite a bit, but that was about it for the highlight film. Carl was rarely in a position to deliver the ball to his fleet wide receivers, and nothing else worked much at all.

From the bench, Billy could see that there was no way Tucker had a chance. Maybe if they'd been more organized, more unified. But you couldn't work out those kind of problems on the field against a team like Cranbrook. Billy figured that he could've done as well or better than Carl in that second half, but he sure didn't think he could've beaten Cranbrook.

It was a bruised, battered, and thoroughly demoralized Tucker team that finally plodded off the field. Who knows what the score was, Billy thought. Some substitute started to announce it, and Norm clapped a hand over the guy's mouth. "I don't want to know," he said, and the sentiment was echoed by other starters.

In the locker room, Doc spoke to the team. "The second half was a lot better," he announced. Most kids just stared at him, and the coach held up a hand. "I know what you're thinking. We weren't successful. But we cranked up the intensity level, we executed better, and we never quit. You guys gave it all you had that half, and I can't ask for any more than that. Cranbrook just played great—much better than the first half. That's a whale of a team we saw out there. Especially for so early in the season. Give them some credit; they made us look bad, and we're *not*. So go ahead and get mad. You got whipped and you should be upset. But keep your head up about that second half—you've got nothing to be ashamed of."

Nonetheless, there were a lot of bowed heads in the showers, and not a joke to be heard around the lockers.

SEVEN

Tucker, Massachusetts was a town of about ten thousand, tucked away just northwest of the Berkshire Mountains. Originally a nineteenth century mill town, Tucker was still an industrial community with a number of small factories. The Heritage Printing Plant was the largest of these; Billy's father worked there.

Once a year, right around the time school started, the plant held an employees' picnic. It was a major town event, open to everyone. The picnic was held all Saturday afternoon on the shores of Lake Grover, and the Tibbs family always attended. It was the kind of scene that brought out the kid in grown-ups, the romance in girls, and the appetite in boys. When Billy arrived at the lake at around twelve-thirty, he headed straight to the food area.

Tony was already there, munching on an ear of corn and surveying the arriving crowd. He was thinner than he'd been, and there were dark circles under his eyes.

"Hey Tony! How's it going?" Billy asked.

"It's going," Tony replied noncommitally. He ate corn on the cob in typewriter fashion—polishing off one set of horizontal rows before rolling the corn to the next.

"Do you think anybody eats corn at random?" Billy asked as he grabbed an ear from a nearby picnic table.

Tony glanced down at his food as though he'd forgotten it was there. "I doubt it," he replied, and looked up grinning.

Billy smiled back and peered around. Most people nearby were wearing jeans and sweaters, since the sun hadn't shown up yet and the Massachusetts late summers were cool when it was overcast. Tony was wearing classy khaki pants and a green chamois shirt.

"Aren't you entered in anything this year?" Billy asked his friend.

"Sure."

"You're going to wreck those pants."

"But I'll look good doing it, my man," Tony answered.

"And maybe Sue Fennick will notice."

"You never know." The boys grinned at each other again.

"So what's the word on the case?" Billy queried.

"We've got a lawyer now—Pete Reiser's dad. And he says, no matter what, I won't have to go to work camp or anything, so that's a relief. But even community service or a fine would probably go on my permanent record. Sometimes they let you wipe out the record by being clean during your probation, but he doesn't think we can get that."

"So you're pleading guilty, Tony?"

"No, no. It just doesn't look good. My dad says that if I can picture the worst and accept it, then I can handle whatever happens."

"That's easy for him to say."

"Yeah. But he's really been standing by me on this, Billy."

Stan Flender wandered up, holding a corn dog on a stick as though it were from another planet. "How do you eat these things?" he asked.

"Hmm," Billy answered. "Let me see. I think you put it in your mouth and bite it—kind of like most food, Stan."

Flender smiled. "Well, really I was just making sure it *was* food. This is my first picnic, you know. I'm still learning the ropes."

"I recommend the corn on the cob," Tony told the reporter.

"Too healthy," Stan Flender responded. "Picnics are supposed to be decadent. You have to find food so grotesque that even the ants don't want it."

"I think you've succeeded," Billy said, looking at the corn dog. "I haven't eaten one of those things in years."

"They cause cancer in rats," Tony added.

"Everything causes cancer in rats," Flender pointed out. "But let me switch topics for a minute. I think I've figured out the way to clear you, Tony."

"What?"

"All we have to do is catch the guy that really did it."

"Go ahead. Feel free." Tony had switched back to his zombie voice. "The police couldn't do it, but I'm sure you're better trained in detective work, huh? You've been watching too much TV. Excuse me," Tony turned and stomped away. Billy and Stan Flender looked at each other in bewilderment.

"I guess he's still pretty upset," Billy said. "Sorry about that."

"It's my fault," Flender replied. "Flirting with hope is a dangerous thing when you're feeling trapped."

Billy nodded, but he wasn't listening. He couldn't help feeling that Tony was right.

An hour later, the lakeshore was teeming with people. It seemed to Billy as though everyone he knew was at the picnic somewhere. He'd spotted all three football coaches, his teachers, the whole football team, all the cheerleaders, and lots of other kids from school. There were students from Dewey Prep, too, the private school just outside of town. Billy recognized several that had been on their football team last year. Since the next preseason game—the last one before the season home opener—was at Dewey, he watched these guys carefully.

"Remember them?" Norm asked from his perch on a stump. Billy sat cross-legged on the grass next to him, munching on an ice-cream sandwich. The Dewey players were standing in line to get drinks.

Billy nodded. "Have you heard if Dewey's good this year?" he asked.

"I don't know. Tobin's good, and there's that Polish guy with that name I can never remember."

"Ochwat."

"Yeah, that's it. He's a hell of a linebacker."

"I guess it doesn't matter what kind of team they've got if we don't get our act together," Billy said.

"That's the truth. We could lose to a girls' team right now."

"There aren't any girls' football teams, Norm."

"Oh yeah. Well, it would be interesting, though, wouldn't it?" Norm answered.

"I'm up for it."

It was sunny and warm by the time the teen and adult competitions started. Billy and his dad placed fourth in the three-legged race, losing to Norm and his father for the third straight year.

The adult version of the egg toss was with water balloons for some reason. Everyone paired off, and then each person tossed the balloon to his partner across increasing distances until there was only one team left with an intact balloon. It was easy to spot the losers; one of the partners was always wet and mad. Billy and Norm were partners, alongside a bunch of other football players. Jim Graves and Elwyn Brooks were a team, and there was Jeff and Chip, Matt Kildare and Steve Wainwright, Roger and Ray, Marshall and Carl, and Buck and somebody even bigger and tougher-looking than him named Vince. There were lots of other teams, too—the water balloon toss was one of the most popular contests. But all the Tucker football players were grouped near each other, standing a few feet apart from their partners.

Billy and Norm didn't have any problems the first few rounds. But no one else did, either. At about eight feet apart, teams started messing up. At twelve feet, there was only a third of the starting teams left, although all the football players except Marshall and Carl were still in. Marshall had flung his balloon about fifty feet straight up in the air to Carl, then ran and hid.

A few rounds later, after Billy had thrown his balloon back at Norm, he noticed another one moving across his field of vision. It came from his right and was heading for Buck, who took it on the forehead with a grunt of surprise. The balloon exploded and water blasted him.

"Sorry!" Kirk Tobin called.

"You're going to be a lot sorrier!" Buck shouted, and he started after the Dewey player. Tobin stood his ground, waiting on the balls of his feet, his hands clenched. It was clear to Billy that he'd thrown the balloon on purpose, hoping to provoke a fight. Fortunately, Vince grabbed Buck from behind, pinning his arms, and then Ray and Roger helped hold him.

Tobin stared at the Tucker players with a mocking smile. "I guess we lose. Isn't that a shame?" he said in a gravelly voice loaded with sarcasm. "And we didn't even get a chance to get wet. Think of the fun we missed out on." Kirk and his partner sauntered off, leaving Buck fuming and still struggling to get free.

At that moment, Grant Samuels showed up, misinterpreted the situation completely, and lumbered over to Vince and Buck.

"That's enough!" he shouted, weaving on his feet. "No fighting!" His voice was slurred and overly loud. For a few seconds, he tried to pry Buck's buddy off of him.

"Go lie down, friend," Vince told Grant. "We're just taking care of business here. It's cool."

"No!" Grant brayed, pulling harder on the guy's shoulder and almost falling. Vince shrugged him off, his tattooed arms still clamped around the enraged lineman. For a moment, Grant seemed confused, then Billy saw his eyes focus and harden, and he clambered to his feet. With a roar, he smashed into Vince's back, toppling all the boys. Vince scrambled to his feet and punched the drunk coach in the gut. As Grant grabbed his midsection and stumbled to his knees, a bunch of men from the plant rushed in and grabbed everyone.

Doc arrived a few minutes later. His face was so tight that it looked as though the skin would split and reveal the bones underneath. His expression wasn't exactly anger, and it wasn't exactly disappointment—mostly Doc seemed incredibly stressed. Kind of tense and tired at the same time.

Grant was still trying to fight, yelling curses and carrying on like a maniac when Doc began talking to him. A few minutes later the two men walked away calmly, Grant leaning on his father's shoulders for support. Doc was bowed under the weight of his big son, but no one offered to help.

To Billy, the whole thing was like a scene out of a movie. It didn't seem real at all. And the rest of the balloon toss was completely anticlimactic. Norm got wet, all the football players eventually lost, and some women from the printing division won. As he did every year, the judge pretended to throw a bucket of water on the winners. The women knew what was going on and pretended to be scared, finally letting the confetti from the bucket rain on them with good-natured smiles.

Later, when the live music began, Billy sat with Jennifer Saltz, the girl from his homeroom who was always so friendly to him. She was wearing jeans and a pretty, green embroidered blouse.

"You look nice," Billy told her. He was nervous, but it wasn't too bad.

"Thanks," Jennifer said.

"Are you having a good time?" he asked after a pause. It was the only thing he could think of to say.

"Oh yes. Are you?"

"Sure. I guess so. I don't think it's as good as last year, though," Billy said.

"Why not?" Jennifer asked, smiling at him. She had a beautiful smile.

Billy couldn't smell her hair but he remembered how it smelled, and for a moment he was tongue-tied. "I guess I'm still shook up about the fight," he finally answered. "That drunk guy was one of our coaches, you know. What a mess. And I guess I'm getting a little old for some of the activities here," Billy added.

"I know what you mean, but I still enjoy the picnic a lot—just in different ways," Jennifer replied.

"Oh yeah—me, too. I really like it."

Before Billy could say anything else, Matt came up and asked Jennifer to dance. She gave Billy one more smile and then polkaed off into the swarm of dancers, looking excited to have been asked by a senior football player.

Mr. Muscatini, the principal, of all people, took Jennifer's chair next to Billy.

"So how's the team looking, Mr. Tibbs?" he asked. He always addressed his students with mister and miss, and never used first names.

"Not so hot, sir," Billy told him, caught off guard. "I hope we don't disappoint the school this year."

"Don't worry about that." The bearish man wagged a finger as he spoke. "You boys always do great against those bigger schools, win or lose. What did you think of that ruckus earlier?"

"It was . . . uh, unfortunate," Billy stammered. The principal was making him nervous with all these questions. He'd never really had a conversation with Muscatini before; it was hard to forget that the man was the ultimate authority at Tucker High.

Mr. Muscatini nodded seriously, as though Billy had provided him with some important insight. "Well, I don't want to waste a seat that somebody a whole lot prettier could be sitting in." He rose and slapped the sophomore on the back. "Hang in there. You're going to be a great one some day," he asserted.

The encouragement and praise felt good, but Billy knew that the principal didn't know a whole lot about football. After years of attending all the games, Muscatini was still apt to cheer wildly at the wrong moment. It was funny. As the principal, he was very sharp—no one ever got away with anything. But as a fan, he was completely inept.

At the end of the picnic, there was an awards ceremony. The warehouse division won the overall title and were completely ungracious about it. The guy that accepted the giant trophy said that they couldn't have done it without the "inferior efforts of the pathetic other divisions." Predictably, one third of the audience laughed, and two thirds booed. Next, the president of the company got up and made an incredibly boring speech about productivity and "the American way of life" (although he never said what that was).

By the times the Tibbs left, Billy was exhausted. He'd had fun, but he was still glad the picnics were held only once a year.

EIGHT

The following Monday, football practice began with a meeting in the locker room. The players sat on benches and on the floor, grouped in front of Doc, who stood in the doorway of his office. John Dunheim wasn't around and Billy wondered why. Grant Samuels wasn't there either; it turned out that the meeting was about him, though.

Doc apologized to the team for his son's behavior at the picnic, and announced that Grant would no longer be coaching at Tucker. The head coach was very businesslike at first, speaking rapidly in a smooth, clear voice. Then, as Doc continued talking, he had to search for words and his voice became husky. He said that Grant had an incurable disease—alcoholism—and that he hadn't learned to control it yet. Doc took the blame for hiring him under these circumstances. He also assumed responsibility for cutting the assistant coach too much slack. If he hadn't been his son, Doc admitted, Grant would've lost his job after the Vets' Hall incident. It was a big mistake to tell the players not to drink, and then have an alcoholic working with the team.

"I know that all of this has been distracting to you as football players," Doc finished. He ran a hand through his black hair and looked up at the ceiling. "But let's try to put it behind us and pull together. Jeff, take the team down to the field."

As the players reached the practice field and began stretching, Coach Dunheim arrived, wearing jeans and a green Tucker sweatshirt. "Sorry I'm late, guys," he called. "I need to make a few announcements while you warm up." His tone of voice was a little different than usual, too. Maybe more assertive, or more energetic.

"With Grant gone, we've shifted the coaching responsibilities," Dunheim announced. "I'll be in charge of the defense and Doc'll run the offense and the special teams. I'm sorry we're forcing you to make adjustments at this point in the season, but that's just the way it is. I don't regret Grant having been a coach here—let me make that clear. I think we all learned a lot from him. For your information, he's moving back to Springfield and he's going to undergo treatment there. He said to wish you all good luck."

While the coach spoke, the team finished stretching. It was a warm day; it wasn't hard to get loose.

"Now let's get going on our calisthenics," Dunheim said. "Who wants to lead them today? Somebody different . . . Let's see. How about Buck?"

The whole team groaned. Buck Young had led them once before, turning the warm-up into a test of wills—his against the team's. This time, he was at it again. Buck did jumping jacks at twice the regular speed and push-ups until Billy's arms were ready to fall off.

"What's the matter?" he'd taunt. "Can't keep up with a lineman?"

The team warmed up emotionally, as well as physically, with Buck in charge. By the time the calisthenics were through, and Doc had joined the practice, everyone was angry. Even mild-mannered guys like Jim Grover and Elwyn Brooks were overly hostile. If looks could kill, Buck would have been dead thirty times over.

The first drill took advantage of this situation. The offense, with all the first-stringers in and Carl at quarterback, ran the same play over and over—fullback off-tackle: Chip through the number four hole. There was a lot of good hitting; you could hear the pads popping from the sideline, and Buck got knocked down by practically everyone.

Next, everyone participated in a kickoff drill, regardless of their usual position. Running all the way down the field every few minutes was exhausting, and Billy wasn't accustomed to blocking or tackling at full-speed. It was brutal. It felt as if it was about a hundred degrees inside his equipment.

From kickoffs, the team moved on to running pass patterns against defensive backs. The coaches had everyone take a turn as a receiver; when one of the linemen would catch a pass, he'd whoop it up and spike the ball. It was fun to watch. And Billy guessed that doing the drills together—linemen and all—was good for the team right then.

The sophomore quarterback was in his element during this part of practice. At one point, he rifled sixteen straight passes right on the money, although Ray and Brad dropped theirs. It was so easy, Billy thought, when there were no plays to call and no line was rushing them.

After a while, Norm yelled out that he wanted to see Billy and Carl running patterns, too. The coaches agreed and Billy lined up to take a turn at receiver. He was planning to wiggle his knees and dunk the ball backwards after he caught it, but it didn't work out that way. Billy ran a fifteen-yard buttonhook and whirled to receive the ball. Before he could react, the hard-thrown ball hit him in the stomach. More surprised than hurt, he fell over backward, awkwardly grabbing for the football, which he missed. The team laughed uproariously as Billy sat on the turf and glared at Carl. The knowing smile on the senior's face told him that the timing of the pass had been off on purpose.

When it was Billy's turn to throw to Carl, he fired the ball as hard as he could at his rival's butt, but Carl danced out of the way. The team laughed again. Each succeeding turn, Carl bested Billy in their efforts to make the other look foolish. To Billy's surprise the coaches let it go on.

Finally, practice ended with wind sprints, something they hadn't done in a long time. It wasn't fun.

After they'd showered and dressed, Stan Flender singled out Billy and Norm in the locker room. The reporter had been hanging around taking notes during the practice, but he wasn't after information for the newspaper now.

"Look, you guys," he said earnestly. "I got you off by yourselves because I need your help clearing Tony."

"What's it to you?" Norm asked. They were standing outside the back door of the locker room, and the sophomore linebacker crossed his arms as he leaned against the brick wall.

"I'm sure he's not guilty," Flender asserted.

"So?"

"So I can't stand by and let him get in trouble for something he didn't do."

"What can we do?" Billy asked. "Like Tony said at the picnic, we're not detectives."

"Have you guys got a few minutes?" Stan asked. "There's something I want you to see. How about we ride over to the Arcadia Diner and talk things over?"

Billy looked at Norm, who nodded. "It couldn't hurt," Norm said, "but I've got to get home soon."

A short time later, Flender pulled up in front of the Arcadia, an old-fashioned greasy spoon near the high school on the south end of Main Street. Almost all the light bulbs in its garish sign were burned out, and the landscaping around the small building consisted of dust or mud, depending on the weather. Hardly anyone besides kids from Tucker went there anymore. But the Arcadia let you nurse a soda for an hour if you wanted to, and burgers were decent.

Flender, Norm, and Billy grabbed a booth in the back corner and ordered sodas from the tired-looking waitress. "Take a look at this," Stan said, spreading a note on the table. "I found this taped to my windshield this morning."

"Dear Mr. Flender," the note read. "I know who vandalized your car, and it wasn't Tony LaRico or anyone else on the football team. It wouldn't be right for me to say any more, but it wouldn't be right for me to stay quiet, either. So you know I'm for real about this, check with the police about the type of paint that was used. It was mustard yellow #2 made by United Paint Company and a crank wouldn't know that. Please do what you can to help."

There was no signature but whoever had written the note had scrawled a big X on the bottom of the page.

"This is great," Norm exclaimed after reading it. "The police'll have to let Tony off now."

"No. I contacted them this afternoon," Stan Flender answered. The boys' faces fell. "Even though the kind of paint was right, they still think they've got a good case against Tony. I couldn't even get them to re-open the investigation."

"Why not?" Billy asked. "Doesn't this letter prove anything?"

"They say that anyone could've written it that knows about paint or had access to the police investigation. In fact, Officer Neal figured that Tony's brother had probably sent the note."

"We can get a handwriting sample and prove he didn't," Billy pointed out.

"Then they'd figure it was his cousin. They're just not interested, guys. So it's up to us."

Flender leaned across the Formica tabletop.

"Have you guys got any ideas about who would profit from Tony getting in trouble?"

"The third-string linebacker?" Norm tried. This was a slow junior who was one of the nicest guys on the team. "Naw. It's not Brian."

"No way," Billy agreed. "Maybe it wasn't somebody trying to get Tony. Maybe they were just after you, Stan."

"Maybe. But that doesn't help us much. Everyone at Tucker High hated my guts that day."

"Yeah. That's true," Norm said agreeably. "Who repainted your car? Maybe they were after more business."

Stan smiled. "Maybe it was my mother. I haven't called home in weeks."

The boys grinned and then there was a pause while the waitress delivered their sodas.

"So what can we do?" Billy asked, feeling pretty frustrated about the whole thing.

"Let me ask you this," Stan answered. "You said the Tiger looked familiar to you, right?"

"Yeah."

"Now that we've eliminated team members from suspicion, maybe you can remember where you saw someone who moved like that," Flender told him. "Who else besides football players would you have seen running sometime?"

"I don't know. I can't think of anyone."

"Maybe around your neighborhood?" Norm tried.

"Or on one of the other sports teams?" Stan asked.

"No," Billy replied. "I'm just drawing a blank."

"All right, guys." Stan leaned back against the

red vinyl. "I'll check out the paint angle—see where they sell this brand, and if anyone bought any recently. You two keep your eyes and ears open at school, and we'll meet again if anyone comes up with anything."

"Sounds good," Billy agreed. Norm nodded as he finished his drink.

"I'll give this note to Tony's lawyer," Stan continued. "It'll help at the hearing, I'm sure. Ready to go?"

Billy was thoughtful as Stan drove them home. Maybe whoever had written the note would step forward at Tony's hearing. He figured that was about as likely as Doc naming him first-string quarterback.

NINE

Dewey Prep was a private boys' school that had once had a good reputation, but was now a dumping ground for rich kids with problems. Most came from New York City, and were instantly identifiable by their accents and trendy clothes. And the older students drove Porsches and BMWs instead of old Dodge Darts and Ford Falcons.

The Dewey campus was composed of a half dozen old stone buildings, spread out on lots of green acreage, with majestic, gnarly trees.

The visitors' locker room at Dewey was carpeted, had chairs instead of benches, and a water cooler instead of fountains. The Tucker players made a lot of remarks about the unaccustomed luxuries. Marshall thought that the place needed chandeliers, and Matt wanted masseuses, but generally the team managed to adjust.

As Billy stretched next to Norm and Roger Critchfield, he watched the Dewey team warm up across the midfield stripe. Aside from Kirk Tobin, the fullback, and Phil Ochwat, the linebacker, Dewey's players were smaller than Tucker's. That was a switch. They had a lot of players, though— at least ten more than the Tigers.

The old wooden bleachers were mobbed with Dewey students, which struck Billy as odd until he remembered that attendance at football games—even preseason ones—was compulsory at the private school. The busload of Tucker cheerleaders and supporters came late and had to stand on the sidelines. Billy saw Mr. Muscatini and Tony in the crowd as he finished his calisthenics and headed for the bench.

He still hadn't gotten used to not playing. It seemed to Billy that he just hadn't been given enough opportunities to show what he could do. Didn't the coaches know what it was like to come in at the end of a scrimmage when everyone was tired and the outcome of the game had already been decided? That wasn't a fair test of his abilities at all. And in practice, he was usually stuck with the second-stringers. How could he look good handing off to a slow-footed freshman or passing to a guy with bad hands?

As Dewey kicked off to start the game, Billy tried to let go of his thoughts and be in the present tense. He'd been working on his technique off and on ever since Robert House's lecture. As usual it didn't work; he forgot about his breathing as soon as Roger hauled in the kick.

The Tucker halfback brought the ball back to the thirty-six with some nifty running. Carl took over and called a pitchout to Chip, who rambled for five yards until Ochwat blasted him. That guy

sure could hit. Another run netted three yards,
and then Carl ran on a play that should've gone
for ten or twelve yards, but the slow senior only
got five. Still, it was enough for a first down, and
it gave the Tiger fans something to cheer about.
On the next play, Carl ran a play-action fake and
tossed a safe pass to the tight end in the flat. Pete
Reiser took off behind the blocking of Buck and
Brad, and wasn't brought down until he'd gar-
nered another first down at Dewey's forty-yard
line.

Next, Tucker ran Roger off-tackle and gained
four yards, so it was third and six. Carl called the
square-out pattern, with Chip as a safety valve
from the back field. But Ochwat blitzed and Roger
couldn't handle him. Carl did his best to dodge the
big middle linebacker, but was sacked hard for a
five yard loss. He bounced up, swearing a mile a
minute. So Marshall came in to punt. The deep
snap to the lanky junior was wobbly and high, and
it was all Marshall could do to hang on to the ball.
He got away a hurried kick that shanked out of
bounds on Dewey's twenty-five-yard line. The defense trotted out to try to stop the home team's
first drive.

Mostly the Dewey quarterback gave the ball to
Tobin. The smaller players blocked well for him,
and he ran for four or five yards a crack. On Tucker's sixteen-yard-line, Tobin tore through a big
hole up the middle, and then shook off Jeff Porter
and sidestepped John Bucek. He went into the end
zone with Steven Wainwright holding onto an ankle and Joe Sidney around his waist. Tobin was an
incredible athlete. Also, an incredible jerk. After
he scored, he threw the football at Steve and el-

bowed Joe in the gut. Billy could never understand why anyone got vicious after a successful play. It just seemed dumb. He said something about it to Chip Moorehead.

"Tobin's always been like that," the senior answered. "I played with him in junior high. He's got a chip on his shoulder as big as his head. It's a shame. Kirk could've really gone on to some big things if he wasn't such a pain. You should've seen him two years ago. He's been injured off and on last year and during preseason. Remember when he came up lame in last year's game at Tucker? But when he was a sophomore, he gained one hundred sixty yards against us. I think he scored four touchdowns."

"Whoa." Billy was impressed.

The extra point made it 7–0 and the kickoff return netted Tucker a decent field position on the thirty-eight. Roger was looking good today, Billy thought. But the offense stalled at midfield after one first down, and Marshall had to punt. After the return, Tucker managed to stop Dewey, gang-tackling Tobin for only two yards on a third and three situation.

After the home team's punt, Carl tried again from the forty-one. He ran a quarterback draw first, which really fooled the defense, but only gained three yards. Carl was just too slow to make a play like that go for much, Billy figured. When the senior dropped back to pass on the next play, his blocking held up well and he threw to Pete. The tight end rambled for six yards. Third and one.

"What would you call?" Norm asked Billy.

"I'd give it to Roger," Billy replied. "He's looking good."

"I'd fake it to him and throw the bomb," Norm said. "If I had an arm, I mean."

"Doc would kill you," Billy told him.

Carl did fake to Roger, but he pivoted and handed off to Chip, who skirted the big pileup at the line and sprinted around the end for fourteen yards. He would've gotten more, but the Dewey safety made a really nice tackle, driving his shoulder into Chip's thighs, practically lifting him off the ground. A Dewey lineman was injured on the play and there was an official's time-out while he was attended to.

"We're looking a little better," Billy said to Norm.

"Yeah, I guess," the linebacker responded. "But this is just Dewey. They've only got two good players."

Billy shook his head. "I don't know," he said. "The whole team blocks and tackles well."

"Look," Norm replied. "It's one thing to watch it from here, but I've been out there. Dewey's nothing. We're just making them look good."

Billy nodded, stung by his friend's remark. It was true that you couldn't know the whole story from the bench or the bleachers. Here he was, watching a slower quarterback with a worse arm try to beat a small, private school that shouldn't even have had a chance to score. Great. He might as well stop pretending he was really a part of the team and accept that he was a spectator who just happened to wear a football uniform.

Roger ran for five on the next play, and then Carl tried to hit Matt over the middle, but a Dewey cornerback tipped the ball away. The Tucker quarterback tried to pass to John on third and five, but underthrew the ball badly, nearly giving up an interception. As Marshall punted again, Billy saw Doc talking animatedly to Carl at the other end of the bench. Billy didn't think his rival's play selection had been very good; he hoped that Doc was criticizing it.

Norm got up to go in on defense. "Hang in there," he said, slapping Billy on the helmet.

Tobin charged up the middle again, and although Jeff and Norm met him at the line, the big fullback's momentum carried him for four before he came down. Ten plays later, Dewey scored on a two-yard plunge, and after an unsatisfying Tucker drive that was floundering as the half time whistle blew, the Tigers went into the locker room on the wrong end of a 14–0 score.

The coaches didn't seem to know what to say. Doc and Dunheim talked about a lot of stuff, but none of it really mattered. The players sat in their chairs, sipping their water-cooler water, listening halfheartedly.

Billy was totally depressed. The guys that had played felt bad, but at least they'd been part of it. Billy felt isolated, his clean orange uniform separating him from the real players. It seemed to make him invisible; nobody had anything to say to him. When the coaches finished talking, he just sat as conversations floated around him.

"What did that tackle feel like?" someone asked Chip.

"Did you get a load of the nose on that ref?" another player said.

It was like a foreign language to Billy. Nothing too interesting had happened on the bench. Nothing ever would.

The beginning of the second half was more of the same. Billy sat and watched Dewey run for two more touchdowns as Carl and the Tucker starters spun their wheels. Every now and then they'd get something going, but the drive would bog down. A fumble and an interception didn't help. With four minutes left, a field goal was all Tucker had to show for its trouble. It was 28–3 against the only really easy team on the schedule.

Billy was startled out of his mood when Doc called his name with three minutes left. He ran over to the head coach, who told him to go into the game and open up the offense.

"Get us a touchdown," Doc said. "I don't care how."

Billy glared at the coach for a moment, then nodded and ran onto the field. The ball was on Tucker's twenty-six-yard line.

"Let's go for it," he told the team in the huddle. "Play sixteen on first sound, and I want to see some pass-blocking." He was too angry to feel nervous. It was low class for Doc to throw him in just for trash time. A quick touchdown would show the stubborn old man just what he'd been missing.

Billy took the snap and ran back into the pocket. Only the wide receivers were running patterns, so the pass protection was ample. He watched Matt fake to the side and then sprint deep. Billy stepped up and snapped off a crisp, tight spiral. It was a beautiful throw. Matt didn't have to break stride as he gathered in the long pass on Dewey's forty-yard line, and then turned on the juice. He sailed across the goal line far ahead of the Dewey pursuit.

"One play. Six points," Billy said aloud. Immediately he looked around to see if anyone had heard him. It would've been pretty embarrassing if they had, but the team was already moving on for the extra point. Billy headed back to the bench.

On the sidelines, Doc and Dunheim exchanged a strange glance, and then both congratulated Billy.

"Sensational," Dunheim commented. "That was a collegiate-level pass."

"Billy the Kid," Buck Young proclaimed, grinning. "The fastest gun in the West."

"Western Massachusetts, anyway," Norm added.

Billy shrugged and sat back down on the bench. He was feeling good, but he knew that he wouldn't get back in. Pulling off his helmet, Billy turned to watch Dewey run out the clock.

With twenty seconds left to go, Kirk Tobin came limping out of a pileup, and jogged awkwardly off the field. Suddenly, a circuit in Billy's brain tripped, and he knew who had been in that Tiger suit on the first day of school. The injured figure on the field was loping along in exactly the same way as the Tiger had been that day in the parking lot.

He thought about it in the locker room and on the bus ride back. They'd need to check if Kirk had been hurt back then, and if Dewey had started classes later than Tucker. Offhand, Billy thought that they had. That would leave Tobin free to get the Tucker football team in hot water. The more Billy thought about it, the more plausible it all seemed. It was just the kind of thing that a guy like Tobin would do. And if he'd pressured his little brother Frank to help him, he could've gotten hold of the mascot suit without any problem. As a Tucker band member, Frank would've had access to the closet where the Tiger costume was stored. And Frank probably wrote the anonymous note. It all fit.

At home, Billy called the police right away, and asked for Officer Neal.

"So you think you can positively identify someone by the way they run?" Neal asked after Billy had explained about Tobin.

"Well, not everyone," Billy replied, "but in this case, yes. With that sore leg of his, it's pretty distinctive."

"But you didn't remember until Dewey whipped your team by eighteen points, am I right?"

"That's when I saw Tobin run that way again," Billy protested.

"What about this guy, Frank?" Officer Neal continued. "The evidence you have on him is that he's somebody's brother, right?"

"Look, Officer. Why are you giving me such a hard time?"

"That's my job, Billy. It's nothing personal. If I don't play devil's advocate now, some lawyer will later. I want my arrests to stick."

"Maybe that's why you won't hear anything that helps clear Tony," Billy retorted.

There was a long pause on the line. Finally, Officer Neal said, "Okay, tell me again about seeing Tobin in last year's game."

When the policeman finished his questioning,

Billy asked one of his own. "Are you going to check this out?"

"Of course. This represents an eyewitness account," Neal replied.

"So what are you going to do?" Billy queried.

There was another pause, then the policeman answered in a gentler tone of voice. "I'm sure you know that's none of your business, but I'll tell you anyway. I'm going to check on Kirk Tobin's whereabouts at the time of the crime. I'm going to question Frank Tobin, too, and we'll get a handwriting sample and match it to the note that was sent. I'll probably talk to Kirk's coach and doctor about his leg, and I'll do more checking about the paint. They might sell it at Tobin's Department Store. After that, we'll see."

"That's terrific," Billy exclaimed. "That's just what I would've done."

"Gee, thanks," the officer answered sarcastically. "Are you sure I didn't miss something?"

Billy felt himself grinning. "Sorry about that. I guess I'm just excited that the investigation's open again. It is, isn't it?"

"Yeah, but don't get your hopes up," Neal answered. "Unless we get more evidence, I don't think your I.D. will stand up."

"But I know I'm right."

"Then I know I'll find something," the officer assured him.

Billy hung up the phone, feeling hopeful for the first time since Tony's arrest. Maybe it would just be a matter of days now before the whole mess was settled.

TEN

At school on Monday, it seemed as though everyone Billy met had a few unkind words to say about the football team. School spirit was at an all-time low, and it didn't help that the Tigers were to play their first conference game against Lakeview Free Academy on Friday evening; if the Tigers lost their home opener, there'd be plenty of time to plan a losing season. And pretty good cause, too, Billy figured. Lakeview had a decent sports program for a small prep school, but Tucker had always beat them. The problem was that Lakeview usually beat Dewey—and it seemed like the entire high school enjoyed pointing that out.

In study hall Billy watched while workmen in blue coveralls finished installing new lights in the classroom. The kid sitting next to Billy told him that it was because of a lawsuit brought by an ex-student who was now blind from squinting so much in study hall.

"Yeah, right."

The workers were noisy and kept forgetting that they weren't supposed to swear in front of the students. It was impossible to get any work done. When the new lights finally came on, it was a different world. Everyone was saying things like "I didn't know those tiles were red" and "Phyllis—are you in this study hall, too?" It got out of hand, and while everyone was making jokes and cracking up, a messenger came in with a note that said Billy had to report to Doc's office.

On the way, Billy tried to find out what it was all about, but the freshman who'd brought the note didn't have any idea. "Maybe you're getting kicked off the team," he suggested.

Billy took a mock swipe at his head. "Thanks a lot."

Both coaches were in the office. And Carl Mulbrauer was leaving as Billy arrived. His face was blank—no clue there.

"Come on in," Coach Dunheim said.

Billy walked in tentatively and gingerly sat in the wooden chair in front of Doc's desk. He was very nervous, and he couldn't seem to keep his hands still. The head coach was sitting at his scarred, ancient desk, while Coach Dunheim stood beside him. Behind the two men was a floor-to-ceiling wooden trophy case that was filled with plaques, loving cups, and statues that Doc's team had amassed through the years.

"We've got good news for you," Doc said. His voice didn't sound enthusiastic at all, though. In fact, his whole demeanor seemed depressed. The corners of his mouth were turned down and there were even more furrows than usual in his brow. "Maybe you should tell him, John," Doc suggested to his assistant. "This was really your idea in the first place."

"Sure, Doc. Here's the deal, Billy." Coach Dunheim leaned forward a bit. "As of right now, you're our starting quarterback. Carl's moving down to the second team, and you're the man on Friday."

"Really?" It was hard to believe. "Just like that?"

"It might seem sudden from your point of view," Coach Dunheim explained. "But we've been discussing it all preseason."

Doc shot his assistant a funny look. "That's one way to describe it. You've had a fighter in your corner, Billy, ever since the opening bell. But Grant and I thought that Carl's maturity would pay off. It hasn't. It's probably not his fault, but it's time for a change. I just want to know one thing. Can you handle it?"

"I sure think so. I'm ready." His voice contradicted the certainty of his words; he sounded nervous and unconfident.

"Great," Coach Dunheim replied. "We'll talk more at practice, but I thought it would be good to get used to the idea."

Billy nodded stiffly. "Thanks. It helps."

"Just do your best," Dunheim told him. "And keep in mind that your best is the best this school's got. You're the starting quarterback now and that means a lot."

Billy couldn't help smiling. "You guys really think I'm your best shot?"

"We do," Doc answered. "Don't get me wrong. You wouldn't play a minute if I didn't have confidence in you. Now get back to class and try not to smile continuously for the next two hours."

"Yes, sir." Billy tried to stop smiling but he couldn't. "I'll stop later," he said, and practically ran out of the office. His little escort was waiting to accompany him back to study hall.

"I'm the starting quarterback," Billy told the boy. He had to tell someone; he was bursting with the news.

"Way to go. Can I touch you?" the freshman answered sarcastically.

The sarcasm bounced off Billy. His excitement was way out of control; he was actually shaking. If he'd had a football in his hands, he would've thrown it a mile or two.

Later, in gym class—in fact, it was exactly halfway through a softball game—Billy's excitement turned to pure terror. Suddenly, he couldn't imagine directing a varsity football team. And to make it worse, he knew Doc didn't really want him—Dunheim had talked him into it. Billy could see it happening: He'd go blank in the first huddle and do something totally stupid again. *Only this time the whole world would be watching.*

During the activities period, Billy tried to put things in perspective. The real problem would be the older guys on the team accepting his leadership. He had exactly four days to earn their respect, and it wasn't going to be easy. Carl was popular with almost everyone, and Billy was sure that a lot of the older players would resent a sophomore taking over their friend's position.

To Billy's complete astonishment John Bucek was on his side. "You're a better passer than Carl," he pointed out as the two sat in the bleachers, their books scattered around them. "And you're a better runner. You're faster and you've got more moves. It's really obvious."

"Do you think the other guys think that?" Billy asked.

"A lot of them do. The thing that Carl's got on you is play-calling, that's all. He's always been mediocre when it came to talent."

"You act like calling plays is easy."

"It isn't, but it's learnable." Bucek shrugged and began folding a page of calculus problems into a paper airplane. "You can't teach Carl to run faster or throw farther. Not much, anyway. But the rest of quarterbacking is mostly experience. In math terms, talent is a constant and field savvy is a variable. You see what I mean?"

"Yeah, I guess. Do you really think I'll do all right?" Billy asked.

"Do vertebrae have cell mitochondria? Do quasars pulsate? Does anyone understand it when Ms. Walker explains syntax? And what about the Visigoths? Did they really sack Rome or just temporarily bag it?"

"You are one of the strangest guys I ever met," Billy told the senior.

Bucek launched his plane from the bleachers. "Thank you. You'll do great. Just throw it to me."

"Right."

* * *

Doc announced the change in quarterbacks at the beginning of practice. He stood in the middle of the practice field, his arms crossed and his Red Sox cap pulled low on his sun-worn face. There were murmurs of surprise, and just about everyone turned to watch Billy's reaction.

"The king is dead. Long live the kid," Matt intoned beside him. "Just throw it to me," he told Billy, winking.

Doc was explaining that he was planning to pass a little more with the new quarterback when Chip sidled up on Billy's left. "Just give it to me, Billy. I'll get you yardage."

"He's too slow," Roger said from Billy's right. "Hand off to your halfback a lot. You won't be sorry."

Doc cut off his speech and glared at Roger. "Is there something important you need to share with the team, Critchfield?" he demanded.

"No, sir. Just giving Billy a few pointers."

"I wasn't aware that we'd hired any new coaches. Are you sure you aren't mixed up? Maybe you're supposed to be a player—*listening* when I talk."

At that, Roger shut up and Doc went on with his speech, finally ending by asking Billy to lead the calisthenics.

It was a good way to get used to his new role; Billy ran through the warm-up routine without any problem, and felt a lot better when he was through. It was a drizzly day with threatening thunderclouds blowing in. The storm held off for the rest of the practice, though, which was

mostly a review of fundamentals. Billy spent a
lot of time rehearsing his footwork and handing
off. And the whole team, quarterbacks in-
cluded, took part in blocking and tackling drills.
Carl was on line next to Billy a couple of times,
but refused to catch his eye or say a word. It
must be hard on the big senior, Billy thought.
But Carl had had a fair chance, and if he couldn't
accept the way things were, that was his problem. The practice ended with wind sprints again,
and the team wasn't happy about it.

"Big lungs aren't going to solve our problems," Steven Wainwright complained in the
locker room.

"It's the old-fashioned solution to every problem," Matt said. "Is your team having trouble
with fumbles? Try wind sprints. How about
heartburn or indigestion? Wind sprints. It's always wind sprints with Doc. I'm sick of it, personally."

"Me, too," Pete Reiser agreed.

"Isn't it fun having something to complain
about, though?" Marshall asked.

"NO!" shouted ten guys all at once.

Billy had to smile. The team was united for
the moment, not the least bit concerned about
who was at quarterback or if they'd lost their
last game. It seemed to him that wind sprints
served a purpose—a pretty important one. Doc
was no fool; he didn't rile up the team against
him for the hell of it.

Stan, who'd dropped by and heard the news,
asked Billy for an interview as the sophomore
finished dressing.

"Sure. And I've got something to tell you about Tony, too."

Later, at the Arcadia, Billy told Stan about recognizing Kirk Tobin at the game. The young reporter listened carefully, asking questions now and then. Stan's brown eyes, magnified by the thick lenses of his tortoise-shell glasses, were glued to Billy's face. There were probably only five or six years' difference in their ages, but the reporter could focus his attention in a way that Billy never seemed to manage. He wondered if it was just an age thing and he'd master the trick after a while.

"I wondered why the police called and asked for that note," Flender said when Billy had finished. "Well, this is terrific. Have you told Tony?"

Billy shook his head. "Not yet. I was afraid he'd do something dumb if he knew—to Tobin. He's got a temper sometimes."

"The police will tell him when he's off the hook."

"It should be soon," Billy pointed out.

"I think you handled the situation well. And getting on to my job here, I think you can handle the quarterbacking duties, too. How do you feel about it?"

Stan pulled out a small, spiral pad from his jacket pocket. "Come on, Tibbs. The town of Tucker is going to want to know what their new high school quarterback thinks. So think a little for me."

Billy stared at his soda for a moment before answering. "Well, I guess I'm excited and nervous and a lot of other stuff all at once. I knew they might try me more on the first team, but I sure didn't expect it."

"What would you say your strengths are?"

Billy felt himself redden. "I don't want to brag."

"No, it's okay. I'm asking you. I won't make it look like you're bragging."

"Well, I've got a good arm and I'm pretty fast."

"How about your weaknesses?"

"Inexperience, size, poise, play-calling—you name it, and it's a weakness."

"Which one of those especially worries you?"

"Calling plays. I just can't seem to get it down," Billy answered.

"Couldn't someone else call the plays even if you were the quarterback?"

"I suppose, but it's all part of this leadership thing. I won't really be in charge if I'm not making the decisions."

"Let me ask you this: Do you predict a losing season for the Tigers?"

Billy groaned. The rest of the interview covered familiar ground, and their food arrived just as they finished talking. The fries were wonderful—greasy, but delicious. Stan buried his plateful under tons of ketchup. It looked like the kind of mess that Billy's sister had made at the table when she was three years old.

Later, at dinner, Billy told his family the good news. Alice was ecstatic.

"All right!" the eleven-year-old shouted. "My brother, the star! How much are they going to pay you?"

"Alice, this is high school football—we're amateurs," Billy replied.

"Well, I know that," the redhead responded. "But they could pay you anyway."

"And practice went okay?" Mr. Tibbs asked.

"Yeah. I think everyone got used to the idea of me in there pretty quickly. And it's not like I haven't seen action. I'm just going to have to sound like I know what I'm doing in the huddle."

"Are you scared?" Alice asked.

"Yeah. There's not much time to get ready, and I always get nervous during games. But mostly I guess I'm sick of talking about it. I just got interviewed for the *Herald*. Would it be okay if we talked about something else?"

"Certainly," Mrs. Tibbs replied. "How about school? How are you doing in geometry?"

Billy rolled his eyes and grinned. "I was thinking maybe we could discuss something safe—like dessert."

And that was it for football at dinner. Though Billy didn't particularly want to talk about his math grades, it felt good to get his mind off playing. It crept into his thoughts enough later—during his homework, watching TV, and especially while he was trying to fall asleep. He even dreamt that he was hiked an order of fries instead of a football, and when he tried to pass it, his arm fell off.

ELEVEN

The next day practice began with Billy and the starting offense running plays against the best defensive team that Coach Dunheim could muster. Six of his starters were two-way players, so it was basically only half the regular defense. But the second-string players tended to practice at game intensity, which compensated for their lack of experience.

Doc positioned the offensive team at their own forty-yard line, and after each play they'd return to this line of scrimmage. It was the point where most drives had been stalling in preseason.

Billy began the first huddle by laying down the law. "Let's get a few things straight, guys. Nobody but me talks in my huddle. I call the plays and I'm not interested in any suggestions. If you've got some specific information I should know—like you were open on the last play—tell

me before the huddle, and I'll decide what to
do.'' Billy had rehearsed this speech in his head
during the entire activities period, trying it out
on John Bucek (who had cowered fearfully, hid-
ing behind a notebook when he'd heard it). The
team seemed pretty unimpressed, though. Buck
was scowling, and Ray looked bored. Most everybody else just stood there.

''You know what I mean, right?'' Billy continued. ''Too many cooks spoil the broth. It would
be a mess.''

There was still no reaction.

''Well, what's the matter with everyone?''

Matt raised his hand.

''Yes?'' Billy responded.

''You told us not to talk in the huddle.''

''Oh, yeah.''

Doc's voice cut through. ''Five-yard penalty
for delay of game,'' he brayed.

The eyes of the offensive unit were fixed on
Billy. ''Forget it,'' he said. ''Fifteen on two. Let's
get 'em.''

Billy took the snap from the thirty-five and
handed off to Chip, who blasted through the line
for six yards.

As the quarterback walked back to the huddle
Matt trotted up to him. ''I was open,'' the receiver said.

''It was a *running* play.''

''But you said we should tell you.''

''Give me a break, Matt, huh?''

Billy called for a quarterback draw on the next
play, and he scampered for nine yards before
Norm upended him.

"Nice tackle," he told his buddy as they un-
tangled themselves.

"That play won't work next time," the linebacker replied. "You guys just got lucky."

In the huddle Billy called for the same play.
He could see a few guys exchange uneasy
glances about it, but he was sure he'd catch the
defense by surprise.

He was wrong. Norm and Elwyn Brooks
smeared Billy for a two-yard loss.

"Don't ever listen to the defense," Elwyn told
the quarterback after he'd pulled him to his feet.

Norm winked at Billy, grinning. "Wasn't too
lucky that time, was it?"

"They're right," Chip added en route to the
huddle. He continued talking as the offense
grouped together. "If you react to them instead
of—"

Billy cut him off. "Thirty-six blue on three.
No talking in the huddle." He could see the hurt
on the fullback's face. He knew that Chip was
just trying to help, but it was important to keep
things under control.

The short pass to Bucek went for eight, and
Billy didn't feel bad at all about how he was doing so far.

On the next play, back on the forty-yard line,
Billy and Roger bumped shoulder pads on a
hand-off and the ball came loose. The defense
recovered, and Roger shot a glare at the young
quarterback. Billy wasn't so sure it was his fault,
though. "What happened?" he asked the halfback in the huddle.

Roger just stared at him until Billy remembered his rule. "You have my permission to talk," he said.

"Thank you, Your Highness. Are you sure it won't give the other players ideas, though?"

"Shut up," Jeff Porter told him.

"Give the kid a break," Pete Reiser added.

Billy frowned. "I don't need you guys defending me," he told them angrily. "Let's just forget the whole thing before we get another penalty. Twenty-one blue on first sound."

This was a medium-length pass over the middle to Matt, with Pete and John taking the linebackers to the right on decoy patterns. Billy was still upset and badly overthrew the ball, which landed right in the arms of a very surprised defensive back. Fortunately, the tall sophomore dropped the easy interception.

Billy tried to put the last few plays out of his mind as he prepared for the huddle. He'd probably been passing more than Doc wanted, he figured, so he called for a pitch-out to Chip. Billy did his part and delivered the ball to the fullback, but something went wrong and Chip was nailed after only a yard.

The linebackers blitzed on the next play, two of them hitting Roger in the backfield before he'd built up any momentum. Then the safety blitz caught Billy in the pocket before he could toss a screen pass. Finally getting the picture, Billy ran a keeper play around the right end which bypassed the blitz. He picked up five before being run out of bounds.

It was frustrating to always have to back up and run the next play from the forty-yard line again. It seemed they would never score unless

Billy threw long. He thought about it and decided that he'd set up the defense enough—it
was time to try the bomb.

Matt and John ran fly patterns along their re-
spective sidelines. Both were open and Billy's
protection was good. He felt confident as he
stepped up and released a pass to Bucek on the
right. But once again he overthrew his receiver.
The ball landed just inches beyond Bucek's div-
ing fingers.

"Good call," Jim Grover told Billy between
plays.

"We'll get it next time," Brad Palmer added.

The line really seemed to be on his side, but
Billy was annoyed with himself; he should've hit
Bucek for a touchdown.

"I was open," Matt complained during the
break. He was still huffing and puffing from the
long sprint.

"So was Bucek," Billy answered. "I just
missed him."

Matt stalked off and sat by Roger. They were
the two players who seemed to miss Carl the
most. In fact, after the senior quarterback wandered onto the field during the lull in the action,
the threesome spent the break laughing and ignoring the rest of the team.

Marshall got his mouth in high gear during the
time-out, too, and Billy hoped that the jokes
would stop before play resumed. He needed time
to think, and he couldn't focus with all the chat-
ter going on around him. It didn't get any better
when the drill continued, though. Billy ended up
calling a long series of running plays, just to be
on the safe side. He didn't feel centered enough

to try anything tricky or risky, and most of the running plays worked against the makeshift defense.

Finally, Doc called a halt to the drill, and the team adjourned early to the locker room for some "chalk talk." Doc wanted to introduce several new plays on offense, and Coach Dunheim had a new zone alignment for the defensive secondary.

"I saw a Lakeview scout at the Dewey game," Dunheim explained. "This should mess them up good."

"Is that any way for a school administrator to talk?" Marshall kidded.

"You're right. This should mess them up well," Dunheim replied with a smile.

The team was pretty loose during the skull session; it hadn't been a very tough practice. And watching a blackboard sure beat running wind sprints.

Billy wasn't nearly as tired or troubled that evening as he'd been the night before. He wasn't pleased with his performance at practice. There had been a lot of problems, but at least they were specific things he could work on, instead of vague fears. He was trying to figure out why he was overthrowing so badly when the phone rang. It was Officer Neal.

"I've gotten a lot done," the policeman told Billy. "But you're not going to like what I've found out."

"Why not?"

"Kirk has an excellent alibi. On the day Flender's car was vandalized, Tobin was with two

friends out at the lake, and they back him up on
that. His brother didn't write the note, either."

"Are you sure?"

"The handwriting expert was positive. But
when I talked to Frank Tobin, he was as nervous
as a . . . well, I don't know—he was very nervous, like he knew something."

"He does. He knows his brother did it," Billy
said. "And I don't care who Kirk bullied into
covering for him. The more I think about it, the
more positive I am that he's the one. Did he act
guilty, too?"

"I didn't say guilty, Billy," Neal corrected. "I
said 'nervous.' No, Kirk was cool as a cucumber.
But I've had dealings with him before. He's a
terrific liar—really top-notch—so what he said
doesn't necessarily mean anything."

"But what do *you* think?" Billy persisted. "Do
you still think it was Tony?"

The police officer hesitated before answering.
"To be honest with you, no. I think you're right
about Kirk. But until I get more on him, my
hands are tied. I need some leverage to pry his
brother and his friends off their stories, and I've
got nothing. The paint angle was a dead end,
too."

Billy wasn't going to give up. "What about his
injury? Was Kirk limping back then?"

"Kirk's doctor says it's a trick knee—it comes
and goes—but the injury angle just comes down
to your testimony. And I checked with the pros-
ecutor's office. They say your I.D. won't stick in
a hearing."

Billy was suddenly struck by the fact that Officer Neal was being very frank. "Why are you telling me all this?" he asked.

Neal paused. "I need your help. I've got an idea about how to nail Tobin, but what I need is for you and Tony and Norm to stay out of this— to give me room to operate. I can't discuss any plans right now, but I want you guys to be cool, to act like nothing's happening."

"Oh." Billy couldn't help feeling disappointed.

"And if I need anything else later, it's great to know you're there."

"Yeah," Billy responded glumly. "We're here."

Billy hung up feeling as if he'd just been on a roller coaster. On one hand, he was disappointed that there wasn't a stack of evidence against Tobin. But it was great that Neal was trying to nail him. And it was exciting to be asked to help, but when that turned out to be doing nothing, it was more disappointing than if the subject hadn't come up at all. The worst part was thinking about Tony still having to face a trial for something he hadn't done.

Just before Billy turned in for the night, the phone rang again. It was John Dunheim calling about the first pep rally the next afternoon. At Tucker, Principal Muscatini ran the show personally. The gathering was held in the auditorium during the activities period, and virtually the whole school attended.

"As you know, Billy, the starting quarterback usually makes a speech," the coach told him.

"Holy smokes! I forgot all about that," Billy

replied. "Do you think we could skip it this year?"

"We could, but I don't think it would be a good idea. You can just say that the team's ready and you appreciate the school's support. It doesn't have to be anything elaborate."

"I get awful nervous, Coach. Last year I hid behind all the other substitutes up on stage."

Dunheim chuckled. "I remember. I saw you back there, and I'll tell you something—it didn't inspire me."

"What do you mean?"

"Let me put it this way. Anyone who knows you is going to know how hard it is for you to speak in front of so many people. So when you do it, you're doing something brave and they'll appreciate that. It doesn't matter if you stutter or forget the words. What matters is that you don't back away from something really hard for you to do. That's the quality that a team respects in a quarterback. So what do you think?"

"I think I don't want to be having this conversation," Billy replied. He hesitated a moment, knowing he'd have to give in. "Okay, but I don't guarantee anything. I'll probably make a fool out of myself."

"It's better to have tried, no matter what happens," Dunheim assured him. "Thanks, Billy."

As he put down the phone, Billy realized that now he had something else to worry about. There were only three more days before the game and things were moving a lot faster than he'd wanted.

TWELVE

"Welcome to the best pep rally in the state!" Principal Muscatini shouted into the microphone as the crowd in the auditorium roared back. The football team and coaches sat in folding chairs on the small wooden stage. Everyone just barely fit, and the auditorium in front of them was packed, too. Billy was very conscious of the bright lights shining on him. He felt like a museum display or a piece of food in a deli counter. The guys around him were uncomfortable, too, shifting around in their chairs or coughing nervously. But they were lucky, Billy thought—they didn't have to speak.

"There's no school anywhere that's behind their football team as much as Tucker—am I right?" Principal Muscatini's voice boomed through the PA system.

The school cheered, but Billy thought that they'd cheered louder the year before.

"That's not noise," the burly dark-haired principal scolded. "Let's *really* hear it this time. Who's going to win on Friday?"

"Tucker!" the audience screamed.

"Who?"

"Tucker!" The volume was way up there now and Muscatini looked pleased.

"All right!" Muscatini shouted. "I want to introduce a man now who needs no introduction, and I want to hear your appreciation when he steps up here. Here he is—the winningest coach in Tucker history—Doc Samuels! Let's hear it now!"

The head coach walked up to the microphone, looking a little embarrassed by the cheering, especially when it continued for over thirty seconds. But he seemed touched by it, too. And he looked tired. Billy figured that even after all these years, Doc still got pretty stressed-out this time of year. It wasn't easy for him to speak to the school, either, it seemed.

"Thank you," the older man began haltingly. "On behalf of the team, we all appreciate your being here. I, uh . . . think we're going to have a fine team this year. The boys have been working very hard and hard work pays off. I want to introduce them now, and I think each and every player deserves a hand."

Doc introduced everyone and the crowd dutifully clapped at each name. Then Coach Dunheim introduced the cheerleaders, who couldn't fit on stage and had to do a routine in the aisle. Finally Jeff Porter got up to the microphone. As team captain, he had to give a speech, too.

"We've got a lot of good players this year and we all know we can do much better than we have so far," he said. Then he got nervous. "I guess, uh

. . . I guess we'll try our best." Jeff stood at the microphone, staring blankly at the audience. "Uh . . . Marshall told me a joke to tell, but I don't think I will. I guess . . . er . . . I guess that's it. Thanks." He stumbled back toward his seat, but Dunheim called something to him as the crowd applauded. Reluctantly, Jeff came back to the microphone.

"I'm supposed to introduce the next guy, too," he told the audience. "So here's our starting quarterback—the one, the only—Billy Tibbs. Billy the Kid!"

The crowd cheered wildly, as though Billy's nickname made him worthy of extra acclaim. He'd had no idea that Jeff would say that, and he could feel the blood rushing to his face as he walked hurriedly to the microphone. His foot hit the mike stand and he nearly fell, taking the microphone with him. He was a nervous wreck as he righted the stand and lined up behind it. He couldn't remember a single word of his prepared speech. He was in big trouble.

"Uh . . . thank you," he squeaked. The audience cheered again; they were having fun overreacting to him. When the noise died down, he tried again. "I just want to say that I'll do my blest, and that . . . no, no—I mean my best . . ."

The school hooted and clapped. Billy plunged ahead while they were still carrying on. "And I think we're a good team that's not going to win as much as a lot of people are saying—I mean lose. Lose as much." Billy turned even redder and closed his eyes to concentrate. He couldn't believe this was happening. Finally, the hooting and cheering died down, but when he opened his mouth, nothing came out. Nothing at all. The

crowd sat and waited, finally quiet, but not a word
emerged, no matter how hard he tried. After a
long time—seemingly forever—Billy managed to
squeak out "Thank you" before trotting all the
way off the stage and through the exit doors up
front. Once in the hallway, Billy leaned back
against the closed doors and held his head in his
hands. He could hear the crowd cheering wildly,
but he felt like a complete jerk.

As he heard John Bucek introduced, Billy decided that walking around a bit might cool him
down. He certainly didn't want to go back to the
pep rally. After taking a few slow sips from a water fountain, he decided to head for his locker.

The dimly lit halls were deserted since everyone
was at the pep rally, and as Billy turned a corner
he was surprised to see a figure kneeling in front
of Tony's locker.

"Hey, Tony!" he started to call out, but with a
second look Billy realized it wasn't Tony at all. He
quickly ducked back around the corner and
peeked out at the figure.

Whoever it was was obviously trying to get into
Tony's locker. The figure spun the dial, yanked at
the handle, and kicked at the door, but it didn't
open. Suddenly, the person looked up the hall to
where Billy was standing and realized he was being watched. Billy couldn't make out his face, but
whoever it was jumped up and took off fast down
the hall.

Billy leaped out from behind the corner and
gave chase. The guy was fast, but Billy channeled
all the emotion from the pep rally to his legs and
bit by bit began gaining on him.

The halls echoed with the sound of their pounding feet. As they tore around another corner, Billy drew close enough to the figure to see it was Kirk Tobin. He pushed himself even harder, fired up by the idea that catching Tobin would solve everything. *Doc's wind sprints are paying off,* Billy thought grimly. *I think I can catch him, but can I bring him down?*

As Tobin neared an exit, Billy realized he had to make his move. He launched himself at the back of the fullback's legs and hung on for dear life as Tobin dragged him down the hall. As they reached the door, Tobin turned and raised a massive fist. Billy ducked his head as best he could, tensing himself to receive the blow.

But just then a dull roar came down the hall as a crowd of students emerged from the pep rally. Tobin froze for a moment, surprised, and Billy took the opening to drive forward and topple the Dewey fullback.

Seconds later a crowd had formed around the struggling boys, and Ray Burroughs and Buck Young came to Billy's aid. By the time the first teacher showed up, Kirk Tobin had half of the Tucker Tigers sitting on him.

"Okay, okay," Tobin shouted as Buck twisted his arm. "I did it! I tossed the paint on Flender's car! Just get off me, please!"

Officer Neal arrived a few minutes later and took Tobin into an empty classroom to get a statement while Billy waited outside. When he emerged, the policeman motioned for Billy to come over.

"Well, it looks like Tony's in the clear," Neal said with a smile. "Tobin was worried that the Tigers looked too good, so he thought a little 'bad press' was in order, and what better way to get it than splashing a reporter's car with paint?" Neal laughed. "He says the paint on Tony's bike was an accident, but after I questioned Tobin and his buddies about it, he wanted to make sure Tony's arrest stuck." Neal held up a small can. "This paint was going into Tony's locker, and this note," he said, showing Billy a piece of paper, "was going to be sent to the police tipping them off about the paint. It would have been damning evidence if it had worked."

It seemed as though the whole school watched Tobin get taken away in the police car, although few kids knew why at first.

"What's going on, Billy?" Billy turned as Tony walked up, looking confused.

"You're cleared! Tobin confessed to everything!" Billy shouted.

"All right! Way to go!" Tony grabbed his friend and tried to hug him. Billy wrestled free.

"None of that emotional stuff," he protested, but Norm snuck up behind him and pinned his arms.

"Get him," Norm called, and Tony squeezed Billy until he thought he'd burst.

"Great speech," Norm added.

Within an hour it seemed Billy was an instant hero. Jennifer Saltz gave him a very memorable hug, and he asked her out, too. Billy was shocked when she said yes.

Except for John Bucek telling Billy that he enjoyed the use of irony in the quarterback's "epic presentation," the team reacted to the capture, not the rally. Whether this would last or not, Billy wasn't sure. His failure on stage was burned into his memory; he knew he'd never forget it. Probably as soon as he blew it again, everyone would remember every awful detail. But at practice that day, it was all handshakes and slaps on the back, and it was great to have Tony back on the team.

The next day, at the last practice before the Lakeview game, nothing went right for Billy. Doc ran another drill where the offense worked out against the defense. This time it wasn't full contact, just a half-speed walk-through, but it was easy to tell if the play would have worked. Billy couldn't seem to take the defense by surprise. When he ran a sweep, the defensive backs were right there to help. When he sent Chip or Roger into the line, the linebackers seemed to be stacked up, waiting. In desperation, Billy called for a reverse on one play, but even that fizzled. His arm felt sharp, and he was delivering the ball where he wanted, but most times something would go wrong on pass plays, too. Either the receiver would juggle the ball and drop it, or a lineman would tip the pass on its way out of the pocket. Out of maybe thirty plays, only five or six were really successful.

The offense glumly accepted Billy's leadership. It was as if they knew that mouthing off would only make things worse. But he could see their frustration as his play-calling simply didn't cut it.

Doc interrupted the drill several times to discuss strategy with him, but the head coach stopped short of ever suggesting any specific plays. Obviously, he wanted his young quarterback to learn by doing. Doc even told Billy that the best way to remember something was to make a big mistake with it. He didn't act upset at all by the sputtering

offense; maybe Doc saw it as educational. But Billy
experienced the practice as a disaster—a sign of
things to come. He wasn't going to get any better
at running the offense by the next day. Lakeview
would have an easy time of it if nothing drastic
came along to change things.

After dinner that evening, he lay on his bed and
tried to analyze the situation in a deeper way. He
began by breathing slowly and thoroughly, and for
once he felt as though it really helped. His head
felt clearer than it had in weeks, and he seemed
to be in contact with a calmer place inside him.
Then he looked at the way he'd been thinking
about his plight. The first thing he noticed was his
tendency to blame things on circumstances outside himself. He just didn't feel ready to be in
charge of everything. And then he remembered
Stan Flender's idea of his playing quarterback but
having someone else call the signals. The more he
thought about it, the more he liked the idea. With
that responsibility off his back, he knew he could
do the job. Doc wouldn't be excited by the idea,
but maybe he could talk him into it for just the
first game. Then, when he was feeling more confident, he could step up to calling the plays, too.
It seemed like the ideal solution, as long as Doc
would agree to send in plays.

Billy's first urge was to get on the phone to the
head coach right away. But he lay on his bed and
patiently tried to decide the best way to get the
scheme approved. It would be easy for Doc to say
no over the phone. But in person, Billy felt confident that he could convince Doc that he needed
to do it. He took a few more minutes to think it
over and be sure, and then ran downstairs,

grabbed his coat from the hall closet, and trotted out the front door. It was a cool evening, maybe fifty degrees, but it was pretty—clear and crisp, with lots of stars. Doc lived about ten blocks from Billy in a large ranch house that was surrounded by apple trees. He answered the door in a plain flannel bathrobe, holding a book.

"Sorry to bother you," Billy said. "But I need to talk to you."

"Come on in. I don't mind," the coach told him, his voice softer than at practice. He led Billy down a long, carpeted hallway into a den with knotty pine paneling and several old armchairs.

"I hope I didn't disturb you," Billy began as he settled into a brown leather chair that faced the coach's.

"No. I was just reading. I learned a long time ago that coaching isn't a nine-to-five job," Doc replied, gazing into the fireplace beside him. There wasn't a fire going, but for a second Billy saw Doc looking at one. *The house must hold a lot of memories for the widower,* he figured.

"What are you reading?" Billy asked, curious for the first time about the coach's personal life.

"History, mostly. I've read just about everything there is on the Civil War. Or the War Between the States, depending on where you're from."

"Is that what they call it down south?"

"That's right."

"I didn't know that. I thought it was the Civil War everywhere."

There was a pause then, during which both Billy and Doc seemed to get a little uncomfortable.

"So what's on your mind?" the coach finally asked.

Billy explained his idea, concentrating on how it was the only way he could see himself keeping it together the next day.

"If I can't get the plays sent in, I just don't think we can win. I really don't," Billy finished.

There was another pause, longer than before. Doc sat with his hands folded as he thought over Billy's proposal. His quarterback nervously awaited the verdict, one of his feet tapping arhythmically.

"Son," Doc began. "I can't see me calling the plays for you."

Billy's spirits sank.

Doc held up a hand. "I'm not saying we can't work something out. But there's too much going on out on the field for someone on the sideline to be able to do it properly. None of the data coming in from the players between downs would get incorporated into the decision-making."

"They could run over and tell you what happened," Billy tried. "It could work. I really think so."

"How about this?" Doc asked. "Suppose another player on the field called the signals for you. Could you live with that?"

Billy considered it. "I don't see why not. Do you have someone in mind?"

"Chip Moorehead," Doc answered. "He knows the offense inside and out and he's a level-headed player."

"Would he do it?" Billy asked.

"Chip does whatever I ask him to," Doc replied. "He always has."

Billy blushed, thinking of how he was letting Doc down just by asking to get out of calling the plays.

The coach noticed his discomfort and spoke consolingly. "It's all right, Billy. That was a tactless thing for me to say. I meant that after four years of working with him, I know Chip pretty well. I don't think it'll be a problem. Your situation is completely different."

"I wish we didn't have to do this," Billy said. "I wish I could just get in there and make it work."

"Now that I have more feedback from you," Doc told him, "I think this is a real good idea. You just wouldn't have been able to perform your best with the play-calling hanging over you. So don't feel bad that we're changing things. I'm glad you came over here—it took guts and it makes sense. Now, let's give Chip a call."

The senior fullback agreed to the additional duty, and promised to do extra homework with his playbook that evening. Billy felt tremendously relieved as soon as he heard the news. It was as if all the tension had gone from his muscles. In fact, when he stood to leave, he was actually weak at the knees.

Doc noticed his reaction. "Feel a little better, Billy?" he asked with a laugh.

"Whoa. It's amazing. I feel twenty pounds lighter. Thanks a lot, Coach. I really appreciate this."

"Forget it. Now scat home and get a good night's sleep. Tomorrow we put it together and get rolling."

"Yes, sir. Good night."

Billy ran all the way home, pushing himself as

if he were sprinting the entire distance. Grinning, he slid to a stop in front of his house. He wasn't even winded.

THIRTEEN

The locker room was unusually quiet before the game, and Billy took extra care in putting on his pads and tying his cleats. Doc informed the team that Chip would be calling the signals, and though a couple of guys kidded the fullback about it, there basically wasn't much of a reaction. Then Doc had told the Tigers that he asked three things of them in the game.

"One, I want to see you playing as hard as you possibly can. Two, I want to see you trying to go about things my way—remember your technique. And three, I want you to remember that you're representing the school. I don't want to see any comportment problems out there. That's especially important. Now if we can do the three things, we have a good chance of winning, and nothing to be ashamed of if we don't."

On the field warming up, Billy surveyed the arriving crowd. He saw his family climbing to

their seats in the aluminum bleachers. And Mr.
Muscatini was there, of course, wearing his Tiger hat. He looked like a reject from some quiz
show on TV. Billy lay on his back and stretched
his quadriceps, feeling excitement tingle in his
hands and feet. By the time he'd finished
stretching, the crowd had swelled to capacity.
The bleachers were completely full and new-
comers stood on the sidelines.

Billy had been ignoring the red-and-blue clad
Lakeview Free Academy players at the other end
of the field, but a comment by Norm drew his
eyes to them.

"They look okay," the linebacker judged.

And they did. Lakeview was about the same
size as Tucker, and the Minutemen ran through
their warm-up drills with a fair degree of preci-
sion.

Tucker won the toss and elected to receive.
Roger waited for the kickoff as the crowd buzzed
in anticipation and the cheerleaders shouted his
name. It was a good kick and the halfback
fielded it on the eleven-yard line. He followed
his blockers to the left for a few yards and then
cut upfield through a hole for eight more before
being tackled on the twenty-five. Billy jogged
out to the first huddle. Chip called for a screen
pass to Pete, the tight end. On the count of two,
Ray hiked the ball, and Billy ran back into the
pocket.

"Pass, pass!" the defense called.

Billy pump-faked deep and lofted a short pass
to Pete, who blasted through a cornerback and
picked up seven yards. It was a great start and
the team was jubilant in the huddle. Chip calmed

them down with an upraised hand and called his own number on an end sweep. The big fullback made the play work, even though someone blew their blocking assignment. Chip stiff-armed a Lakeview lineman in order to turn the corner, and then ran for five yards before being forced out of bounds. It was good for a first down on the Tucker thirty-seven.

Billy was still a little nervous, but it wasn't bad. He felt as if he could do his job fine as long as things kept going the way they were.

But then Chip called for a quarterback sneak, and Billy could only get one yard before being dragged down by two big linemen. It seemed like a dumb call to him. His strength wasn't smashing into the line on short-yardage plays, and a sneak wasn't designed for a three-yard pickup anyway. Two unsuccessful plays later, the punting team came in and Billy trotted off.

Lakeview made a fair catch of Marshall's high punt and took over at their twenty-eight-yard line. They looked sharp on their first set of downs, and a few minutes later they were knocking on the door on Tucker's thirty-three-yard line. Lakeview ran a fullback draw on a key third-down play. It fooled the Tucker line-backers for a moment, then Norm and Jeff came up fast and both hit the runner a few yards past the scrimmage line. The officials had to measure, but Lakeview hadn't quite made the first down. Their punter kicked the ball out of bounds on the twelve, and Billy returned with the offense.

This time, Chip's play worked better and Tucker marched up to their opponent's twenty-

two-yard line before encountering stiff resis-
tance. At fourth and two, Doc sent in the field
goal team, which seemed a little optimistic to
Billy, knowing Marshall's leg strength. Sure
enough, the lanky kicker left the field-goal attempt short, and Lakeview took over on their
twenty.

This time, Tucker couldn't stop the visitors.
After a six-minute drive, capped by a fourteen-
yard touchdown pass, it was 7–0 against the Tigers. As far as Billy could tell, the defense was
playing well. Lakeview just took it to them.

On Tucker's next series, Billy managed to get
the team down to Lakeview's eight-yard line before Chip called several odd plays and the drive
bogged down. Marshall put three on the score-
board, though, which pleased the fans, and
astounded Marshall.

The kickoff was a disaster. A pint-sized Lakeview kick returner gathered in the ball on the
thirteen and scooted all the way through the
coverage for a touchdown. Eighty-seven yards
and nobody laid a hand on him. The visitors'
bench went nuts.

The Tucker offense couldn't do anything for
the last few minutes of the half, and it was still
14–3 when they adjourned to the locker room.

During the break, Billy reflected on how
things were going. He was pulling his weight
personally. He hadn't fumbled or thrown an interception. On the other hand, he hadn't pulled
off a big play, either. But that was partly due to
Chip; Billy was feeling pretty frustrated by the
play-calling. Every time Tucker got rolling, it
seemed the fullback called something dumb and

ruined the drive. Of course, Chip was responsible for getting them rolling in the first place, too, so maybe it wasn't fair to be so hard on him. Anyway, Billy didn't think they should be behind 14-3. It seemed like Tucker was better than Lakeview, so something was messed up.

Doc agreed with this point of view. "We can turn this around if we just play our game. We're making mistakes on practically all the important plays—missing blocks, not following our interference, tackling too high. We're a better team than they are. If we just settle down and execute properly on every play, we're going to win. That's all it's going to take—just executing the way we can. So let's see some intensity when we get back out there."

Doc's speech seemed to work. The team was fired up coming back onto the field. Billy noticed that Doc and Coach Dunheim both talked quite a bit with Chip, too, so maybe the play-calling would make more sense in the second half.

Marshall kicked to the speedy Lakeview returner, but this time a sophomore on the Tucker coverage team made a great tackle on the eighteen-yard line. Lakeview ran for a first down and passed for another. Then, at their own forty-two yard line, they coughed up the ball on a fumble. Buck really smashed their fullback, wailing away at him with a forearm, and the ball popped loose right at the line. Elwyn Brooks fell on it and the offense ran in to capitalize on the opportunity.

Chip called for a quarterback sweep, and Billy put a great move on the cornerback, getting five

yards on the play. Then the fullback took a hand-
off up the middle for five more and a first down.
From the thirty-two, Chip called Roger's number
and the halfback gained nine tough yards off-
tackle. So it was second and one.

Billy was getting a sense of how Chip was op-
erating. In an effort to be fair, he was rotating
who was getting the ball. As they went into the
huddle Billy figured that it was his turn again.
He just hoped that Chip didn't call the quarterback sneak. He knew that the Lakeview defense
would be expecting it. Chip looked straight at
him. "Next play is yours, Tibbs." Billy felt a
sinking sensation in his stomach as Chip went
on, "Go for the sneak." For a moment, Billy
toyed with the idea of saying something, but he
realized that having given up the play-calling, he
had no right to interfere now. He'd just have to
make the best of it. Even with the defense
stacked up against it, the sneak could work if it
was executed just right.

Billy took the ball on first sound and plunged
into the line behind Ray, who moved the nose
tackle forward. Billy was buried a second later,
but a measurement proved that the Tigers had
miraculously made the first down. A few plays
later, it was third down and goal to go on the
three. Chip wisely called a time-out to consult
with Doc before choosing a play. This was probably the most important down of the game so far
for Tucker. The fullback returned to the field
and huddled up the offense.

"Twenty-one red on three," Chip barked. This
was one of the new plays that they'd learned
that week. Billy was to misdirect the defense by

running right, then he was supposed to hand off to Roger, who carried the ball to the left. It was a difficult play to execute under pressure. Billy licked his lips nervously and called a few "huts" on the line to try and settle down. They didn't work; he took the snap and started to his right.

The defense moved with him and the play looked good, but when Billy turned to hand the ball to Roger the back just wasn't there. For a second, Billy panicked, then he pivoted and scampered back to the left himself. The blocking was in place for Roger; it would work for him, too. Billy sprinted to the left corner and saw that Matt's man was getting around him on the outside, so he cut in and gave it all he had. At the goal line, the slim quarterback was met by Lakeview's well-built safety, but Billy managed to fall forward for the touchdown. The crowd cheered wildly, and the band struck up an old Rolling Stones tune. The celebration continued through the successful extra-point attempt. It was 14–10 now and the Tigers were coming back.

On the bench, Roger apologized for his mistake and both coaches congratulated the rookie quarterback on his heads-up play. Billy just felt as though Tucker had been lucky. He figured that Chip had called a dumb play again—why try something that risky so close in? It just happened to turn into a touchdown. There was nothing to pat themselves on the back about.

For the next few minutes, neither team executed well, and the ball changed hands several times. Finally Lakeview got their offensive machine in gear and mounted another scoring drive.

Luckily, though, the Lakeview center flubbed the snap and the extra point was no good. So it was 20–10, and there were about five minutes left.

The crowd was quiet, and Billy knew either Tucker would have to get something going soon or the game would be lost. His frustration level was way up there after the last few drives had fizzled due to poor play-calling. He just hoped he could keep his cool on this upcoming, vital series.

The offense took over on their twenty-four-yard line. Roger got the call first and slashed for four. Then Chip muscled his way past a hard-charging linebacker for three more. With a third and three situation facing Tucker, Chip once again called for the quarterback sneak. Something snapped in Billy; enough was enough. He couldn't stand by and let it happen. He knew in his bones that they could never get three on the play.

"Call time-out," he told Chip as the other players broke from the huddle.

"What?"

"Do it. Call time-out. Now." He was fuming.

"Okay, Billy. Be cool. I'll call it."

The two players walked to the sideline, where Doc and John Dunheim met them.

"What's going on?" Doc asked.

"I want to call the plays," Billy answered tersely. "I need to call the plays."

Doc was silent a moment. "How about it, Chip?"

"Sounds good to me," the big fullback answered. "I wasn't too keen on doing it in the first place." Billy studied Chip with surprise.

"You got it, Billy," Doc told him. "Take charge."

In the new huddle, Billy informed the offense that he was running the show now. He didn't even bother to check their reaction. He just called a play.

Billy took the snap and faked to Chip, backpedaling for a play-action pass. Expecting one of Chip's plays, Lakeview's defense was completely fooled; Billy delivered the ball to Matt across the middle and the fleet receiver ran for fourteen yards. It was first and ten at the forty-five.

Billy called a second pass play, this one to Pete, and it clicked for eight yards. Then a pitchout to Chip and a keeper up the middle brought Tucker to the Lakeview thirty-six. Things were looking good, but there wasn't a lot of time left. Billy called for a twenty-yard sideline pattern; whether it was caught or not, the clock would stop. He wanted to save his two remaining timeouts for later.

He wasn't nervous at all as he surveyed the field from behind his pass protection. Instead, energy seemed to flow down his arms and legs. Billy felt as though he could do anything. He stepped up and fired a strike to Bucek, who stepped out of bounds at the fifteen.

Three running plays later, Roger took the ball across for the touchdown. The kick was good, making it 20–17. Now if only the defense could hold Lakeview. Tucker needed to get the ball back with enough time to do something.

Billy kept to himself on the bench. Some of

the guys congratulated him and tried to kid
around but it all bounced off. He'd never felt so
totally focused and he wasn't about to risk losing it. It was as if all his energy was flowing in
the same direction, instead of being scattered.
Billy felt more powerful and confident than he
ever had before.

The defense was fired up, too. After the kickoff return, Norm stopped the Lakeview fullback
cold up the middle. Then the whole line seemed
to be in on the tackle as Lakeview's halfback
tried an end-around. When the visiting quarterback dropped back to pass on third down, Buck
chased him around the backfield, and Steve
Wainwright batted down his hurriedly thrown
pass. The crowd went crazy. The Tucker offense
would have another chance.

Roger returned the Lakeview punt eight
yards, fighting his way out of bounds to stop the
clock. Billy and the offense ran onto the field to
take possession at midfield with a little less than
two and a half minutes to go.

Billy's mouth was dry as he stepped into the
huddle. He had to make everything work perfectly. "Play fifteen on one," he called. The
short sideline pass worked for seven.

"Quarterback draw," he told the team next. It
was odd. He couldn't remember the numbers des-
ignating the play, but it didn't bother him a bit.

"You mean play eleven?" Ray asked.

"Whatever," Billy answered. "I'm going up the
middle and you knock somebody down, okay?"

Ray grinned. "You bet," he said.

After the eleven-yard gain, Billy called a time-
out and used it to explain the series of plays

they'd use without a huddle if time ran short. He found that he didn't need to think about which ones to call; they were there as naturally as if he'd been calling plays all his life. He just wondered how long his luck would hold.

A few more short passes and end sweeps moved Tucker to the Lakeview twenty-six. Next, Billy tried to get it all in one play. He pump-faked from the pocket as Matt ran another short pattern, then watched as the wide receiver slipped behind his man and headed upfield. The pattern took time and Billy was forced to dodge a big lineman before he could unleash his arm. He fired the ball into the back of the end zone, and Matt caught it, but not before he was out of bounds. The crowd went temporarily berserk until they realized that it hadn't been a legal catch. But at least the clock was stopped again.

Tucker needed a first down to keep the drive alive, so Billy pitched out to Roger, who scrambled for five yards but couldn't get out of bounds.

Billy called his last time-out with fifty-four seconds left. It was first and ten on the twenty-one; only a touchdown would win the game, and there was no way Billy was settling for a tie against Lakeview.

After the break, he threw a strike to John on the right sideline for seven, and a buttonhook pass up the middle to Roger. The clock was running after this play, so Tucker hurriedly gathered without a huddle, and Billy overthrew the ball out of bounds past Pete to stop the clock. They were on the five-yard line now, with twelve seconds left.

Billy called for the same play-action pass that

he'd used earlier, but Matt was covered and Billy had to throw the ball away to kill the clock again. So it all came down to one play—one play that needed to net five yards.

There was no time to think about it. Billy took a deep breath, called his play, and positioned himself behind Ray. As he took the snap and backpedaled, the gun went off. He faked the ball to Chip, keeping it on his hip as he drifted away from the action. Lakeview took the bait for a second—they couldn't afford not to. But as Billy began to run for the right corner, the defense shouted, "Bootleg! Bootleg!"

Billy sprinted with everything he had, and a defensive back mirrored him on the other side of the line. It was going to come down to a footrace between the two players. Billy focused on his legs, willing power to them, sending them every ounce of energy he had left. He made the end zone with two inches to spare. Tucker had won!

The noise was deafening as the rest of the Tigers grabbed Billy and hoisted him on their shoulders.

"Billy the Kid! Billy the Kid!" they chanted.

It was like a dream. It was almost too much to handle. Billy could hardly breathe as the fans joined in the rhythmic cheer.

"I guess I've got this nervousness thing licked," he shouted down to Norm and Tony, who were supporting his legs.

"I guess so," Norm shouted back with a grin.

"It's going to be quite a season with Billy the Kid in charge."

The season has just begun, and the Tucker Tigers have a long way to go until Billy Tibbs takes them to the top. The next exciting book in the BLITZ series stars Buck Young, a new powerhouse addition to the team. Don't miss:

BLITZ #2
TOUGH TACKLE